# I DO IN CHOO

## A NOSTALGIC TALE OF LOVE

ANAM A. AHMAD

Invincible Publishers

First published in India in 2019



ISBN : 978-93-88333-51-1

Invincible Publishers

Registered Address: 201A, SAS Tower, Sector 38,
Gurgaon-122003

Printed at Thomson Press (India) LTD

*This book is dedicated to all the lovely women, who have inspired me with their desires and dreams to say,*

*"I Do In Choo!"*

*I am extremely stupefied with the details shared by the author. It gives me immense pleasure to see this mind craft.*

*Best wishes,*
*S.M.Abbas Ahmad*

# Preface

*I Do In Choo is a tale of two lovers from divergent milieus which leaves a nostalgic impact of emotions on the people of Edinburgh, Scotland. Back in the crimson summers of Edinburgh, the city witnessed the romance of Julia & Jack. Julia, a sophisticated girl from an highly affluent family, gets drawn towards Jack, a village lad from North Berwick. Jack is a dexterous guitarist. He came to perform at the internationally renowned Festival of Edinburgh. It is an annual festival of performing arts. He received his invitation from the Festival Director. The International Festival brings together top class performers of music, theatre, opera and dance from around the world. Jack has stupefying skills as a guitarist. He catches the eye of Julia, while waiting for the formalities to be completed. He falls for her the very same minute he sees her. Love at first sight indeed!*

*Like a real gentleman, he wins the heart of his lady with a beautiful and unexpected gesture. Julia is a refined woman. She has a pleasing personality and is quite attractive. She is like any other girl who has her own set of desires, and believes them to come true someday. Well, why not? After all, she is the only daughter to the Richest Man of Scotland: William Theodore, a Scottish Industrialist (one of the pioneers of the industrial revolution on the firth of forth). He was a member of the merchant family involved in the import of Iron from Russia and Sweden.*

*Julia is a simple girl. She has grown up planning her wedding gown and shoes. She is very fond of Jimmy Choo, a Malaysian shoe maker, who makes it big in England. Well known for his craftsmanship, Jimmy Choo was first worn by Lady Diana Spencer (a lesser known royal known name), who became his first high profile patron. Since then, his shoes have been worn by every well-known person. Julia loved these stories of the brand. They left an exclusive, priceless impact on her and since her wedding has always been her most exquisite forethought, she couldn't imagine it without on her favorite shoes.*

*Their love flourishes capturing the hearts of many. But in between this nostalgic tale of love intervenes an unanticipated problem. Back in reality, the expectations of one man puts their love on trial: Julia's proud and arrogant father.*

*Will he give his daughter's hand to someone he believes to be just "ordinary"? Or, will he put him through his test of ability, i.e. can he buy her a pair of shoes from Jimmy Choo? Will he be able to walk her down the aisle in her favorite shoes? Will she blithely say "I do in choo!"*

*Anam A. Ahmad (26th March, 1988) was born in Lucknow, India, to the Royal Family of Awadh. She grew up in Lucknow and settled down in the Capital (Delhi, India) in 2012. She did her schooling from La' Martiniere Girls College, Lucknow. Her previous book was "Marriage the Edition & Anny". Anam is a graduate in Tourism Studies. She was an arts student.*

*She has given seven of her sublime years to the retail industry, working with "Jimmy Choo', the magnificent international luxury brand and exceptional Indian designers including Manish Malhotra, Sabhyasachi, Anushree Reddy, Gaurav Gupta and many more, under the aegis of Aza. Writing is her passion. She had composed 12 English songs, in two hours at the age of 14. She wanted to be a singer like Brittany Spears. Her father gifted the first mike she used for a karaoke system at home. The fun part of writing for her is the detailing of certain aspects of every story. She believes writing is a brain game. How deep she thinks about certain subjects that has any form of meaning or make an extra ordinary sense, catches her interest. She was a professional communicator in the retail industry with her clients and brings similar expertise to her writings. She has a passion for words and she enjoys the gambol of this enlightening treasure. She feels there is nothing more beautiful than spreading love, hope, faith, affection, commitment, wisdom, promise and a dream through the seamless power of words. Having grown up with her mother telling her every time, "what you speak can either make someone happy or completely break them", she has learnt to use the power of words very cautiously. She believes we should choose the right words and the right tone to express ourselves. Today she has realized how important it is to understand this as many of us doesn't realize it, until it's too late. She enjoys writing love stories, while inculcating her observations about human behavior, emotions and experiences. She also writes short stories.*

Jimmy Choo
for
Cinderella

# Acknowledgements

This book is the result of my experience of working for four years with the brand Jimmy Choo. An experience which is truly one of a kind. Many fail to understand how one can love the job they do so much. But yes, I was not only in love with my job, but I have also celebrated each moment spent there. The shoes were bought by the connoisseurs of stories. Yes! I sold stories, not shoes. In the unique craftsmanship, every detail had an expression of a tale attached to it. Royal families, renowned dignitaries and celebrities Either they were looking to become a part of the story or they were wearing a story themselves, crafted by the magnificent boutique of Jimmy Choo. "#I Do In Choo" was a popular concept designed exclusively for the bride;. a special pair of choo to be a part of the most special day of a women's life. I would like to acknowledge Jimmy Choo for this concept which not only gives the ultimate shopping experience to the buyers but also a great selling experience to the employees. The happy faces of my clients and their never-ending excitement while choosing the right shoe for their most important day has inspired me to write "I do in Choo". Thank you! Jimmy Choo.

# Prologue

## *Jack & Julia*

*It was a beautiful morning. Julia, the sleeping beauty, is looking her best while fast asleep. She wakes up to the sound of music. She rubs her eyes and stretches as she sits up. She looks at the window where she feels the music is coming from She walks towards her portico, wearing an alluring wrap from the night. Her hair long and curly, is falling on one side of her shoulders. She looks down and to her surprise Jack is standing like a real-life Romeo, playing the guitar, accompanied by a few other musicians. They were there to wishing the beautiful lady the most amazing morning of her life. Jack plays the guitar and sings for her, a song from 80's written by Steve Perry:*

*'Just a small-town girl*

*Livin' in a lonely world*

*She took the midnight train goin' anywhere*

*Just a city boy*

*Born and raised in south Detroit*

*He took the midnight train goin' anywhere.*

*A singer in a smoky room.*

*A smell of wine and cheap perfume*

*For a smile they can share the night*

*It goes on and on, and on, and on*

*Strangers waiting*
*Up and down the boulevard*
*Their shadows searching in the night*
*Streetlights, people*
*Living just to find emotion*
*Hiding somewhere in the night*
*Working hard to get my fill*
*Everybody wants a thrill*
*Payin' anything to roll the dice*
*Just one more time*
*Some will win, some will lose*
*Some were born to sing the blues*
*Oh, the movie never ends*
*It goes on and on, and on, and on*
*Strangers waiting*
*Up and down the boulevard*
*Their shadows searching in the night*
*Streetlights, people*
*Living just to find emotion*
*Hiding somewhere in the night*
*Don't stop believin'*
*Hold on to the feelin'*
*Streetlights, people*

*Don't stop believin'*

*Hold on*

*Streetlights, people*

*Don't stop believin'*

*Hold on to the feelin'*

*Streetlights, people"*

*Julia can't stop smiling. She rushes down to the veranda, where Jack was playing and singing with other musicians. "Yeaaahh! You are too good, man", comments one of the guests. Julia contains her excitement and walks like a lady towards Jack. She looks into his eyes. He is still, lost in her gaze. Jack whispers, "Can I have privilege of a kiss? Or am I allowed to give you a kiss?" Jack asks Julia this question, with a feverous passion in his voice. Julia looks at him in his eyes. She moves closer and slowly says, "You deserve a kiss, Mr.Rockstar". She makes the first move for her first kiss. It is the most erotic kiss, ever witnessed by the hotel guests and staff.*

# Content

# Foreword

Where do these characters come from? They are completely fictional; they have nothing to do with anyone, living or dead. Julia, Jack and all the characters that are a part of the story are imaginary.

In writing these characters each one of them, I have taken a good amount of time; to detail them and create a believable background story. They add good balance to the script. Jack as a guitarist and Julia as a daughter of the rich industrialist and a wedding planner. Not to forget, Mr. Theodore, the rich industrialist; Candy, Julia's best friend and business partner; Roger, the connection between Jack, Candy & Julia. Similarly, the other characters which move the story have been developed to add flow to the narrative.

I have shared what really being in a relationship and getting married means to a girl. A girl who grows up with a love for dressing up. How important her outfit, accessories and shoes are to her. In expressing Julia as a girl like any one of us, with dreams and desires for the magical kind of wedding she yearns to have, I have laid bare a part of myself. Her love story is nothing less than a fairytale, with her disapproving father who will not agree to her betrothal to a common musician. Jack's unconditional love for her and his overall flirtatious nature, adds a lot of zing to the story. Since it's an old school story, the union of the rich girl and the poor lad, I have tried to make it a little different for all to grasp and enjoy through a modern presentation.

I have shared certain moments, between the two, which I have craved as a woman or have thought for my perfect relationship. Like any other girl, how they would want their man to take them to seventh heaven just by loving them so. I have attempted to detail this in such a way that is personal as well as contemporary..

# Love at First Sight

During the summer in Edinburgh, the road where The Royal Mile is, was lined with shops selling souvenirs, clan tartans and whisky. The road leads to the 16th-century Holyrood Palace, an official royal residence. This is the location of the internationally renowned Edinburgh Festival. It is an annual festival of performing arts, where the world's most renowned artists of music, theatre, opera and dance come to perform. On the one end of the location, there are restaurants in waterside Leith, where they serve all varieties of sea food, from ethnic Scottish seafood to traditional Australian fish and chips. A sophisticated girl from an affluent family was enjoying her cappuccino and reading her copy of Love story by Erich Segal. She has sharp features, an innocent smile and a fair complexion. She is wearing a white Gucci jumpsuit and Prada glares. There is a big tiffany ring on her right index finger and an elegant Cartier watch on her wrist. To the village boy who had come to perform at the festival, this was all visible from a distance .

Jack Denver is a renowned singer and musician in his village, North Berwick. Jack is popularly known as JD. He is a guitarist by profession. His performances are no less than a smooth operator, extremely mesmerizing. Jack had been preparing for this festival since a long time. Standing all day long, waiting for the formalities to get over, Jack's eyes began to wander. His eyes passed by this sophisticated girl, sipping her cappuccino while so involved in the book. From head to toe she was dressed so exclusively. Jack couldn't take his eyes off her, he continued gazing at her, longingly. While turning the page of her book, Julia takes a deep breath and for a wee moment, her eyes catch the attention of Jack's yearning gaze. She is not surprised. Julia gives a royal ignore, with an air of 'as if I care'.

After a few hours of waiting, Jack is called, along with his troop, to perform. He gives the best test performance and as expected he, along with his troop, is shortlisted to perform in the main festival. Laughing and singing, the band walks off the podium, congratulating each other. Jack is trying to figure out if he can still find Julia anywhere, but he cannot find her anywhere around. He walks down, dispirited, hoping for a chance to see her again..

Julia is a young, rich girl with high aspirations. She works as a wedding planner cum match maker with Candy, her best friend from childhood. Candy comes from an upper class family, who runs a small startup as a wedding planner. Julia, who believes that she is perfectly suited for match making. She volunteers for the role. There company was popularly known as "The Velvet Box" all over the UK. Candy's father and Julia's father were friends too. Julia's father, William Theodore, was a Scottish Industrialist who was one of the pioneers of the industrial revolution on the firth of forth. He was a member of the merchant family, involved in the import of iron from Russia and Sweden. At present, he is a top industrialist, seen often with his business partner and best friend, Jeffrey Atkins. Jeffrey is Candy's father, who is a sharp businessman. Jeffrey has a son too, other than his daughter Candy Atkins. Bradley Atkins is the spoiled brat. He is known for two things: for breaking traffic rules and the hearts of many innocent women.

Candy has the event passes for the festival. She shares the passes with her favorite, Julia. "Babe! You have to accompany me to this festival. It's been organized by our client. I can't say, no", she informs Julia. After much discussion, Julia agrees to go to the festival. They leave home by 9:00p.m.). She was dressed like an icon. On reaching the event, they were both escorted by the security to their assigned seat. Centre middle seats from the front. That's what Candy expected and to her surprise those were the seats issued to them. Performances continue one after the other. Finally, the much awaited Band hits the podium. "THE ELECTRIC BASS ORCHESTRA". The host announces the name aloud, "Our next performers..." Julia get's a call on her phone. She leaves the audience and moves out looking for a silent place, where she can answer the call. Jack is standing on the stage, starts playing the guitar. Winning over hearts of the girls sitting in the audience, but he is unaware of the presence of the face he is looking for. Julia could hear the performance of the troop as a faint sound, and couldn't really watch them performing from the back. She disconnects her call and goes back to her seat. However, Jack's performance was over by then. He bowed and left the stage, while Julia smiled at Candy and apologized for leaving her during the show. "You missed such an amazing performance, you have no idea!" informed Candy. With no regrets, Julia enjoys the next performance. While backstage, Jack catches a glimpse of Julia. He shouts "hey, hey, hold that camera. He runs down and is excited to see her sitting in the front row. Jack wants to reach out to her, talk to her. He tries his best but the event organizer called him, that very minute. An annoyed Jack, holds his calm, relaxes himself and says in mind "After the show". The show ends and everyone in the audience begin moving towards the exit. Jack is stuck in the green room with an annoying costume designer, who is relentlessly and shamelessly flirting with him. He pushes him out of the way and reaches the front of the stage. Julia is standing far away, at the exit. The crowd pushes her out and she is out of his sight again. Jack doesn't give up. He run towards the exit, fighting with crowd to let him out. But they were not destined to meet then. Candy's chauffeur gets the 7 series out from the valet. They walk to the car and leave the festival in no time. While giving a look back once, Julia sees the man struggling to find his way out through the crowd of people. She looks at him and thinks, "I have seen him before, but where? "Candy initiates the conversation, "What are you looking at? You seem so lost in your thoughts!" Julia looked down and then straight, "Ah nothing. Just looking at that crazy crowd of people you know how much it scares me". Candy, smiling at Julia, says "Are you tired?" Julia retorts- "Sort of. I'll reach home and hit the bed." Candy brushes Julia's hair "Hmmm. But the only thing that you missed was actually that which you shouldn't have missed. What an electrifying performance by EBO. I so love this guitarist". "Who?" asks Julia with a curious expression, "The guy who played the guitar in the band. You missed it babe", replied Candy. – "Oh, Ok! Looks like you can't get over him", says Julia, with a coy smile.

The night passed. It was quite a lot of fun for the two. As for Jack, he was a little low and tipsy. However, he was happy with the performance given by his troop and him. He has a long next day waiting for him. He was on his way back to his village in North Berwick. Once there, he falls on his bed and begins to go into a deep slumber.

Mr. William Theodore, along with Jeffery Atkins, had the membership of the very popular Golf Club in North Berwick, called the North Berwick Golf Club (NBGC). It is the 13$^{th}$ oldest golf club in the world. It is also the first club in the world to allow female members. Jack's best friend, Roger, is a golf cart attendant at the club. There was a much awaited match being hosted by the only St. Andrews. Invites were sent. Both the industrialists, Mr. Theodore and Mr. Atkins, were two of the most popular participants. Roger invited Jack to experience the match at the NBGC. At the other end of the spectrum, we have Julia & Candy too, in support of their fathers. While sitting in the crowd of people and cheering for their respective players, Julia & Jack were unaware of each other's presence so far. Julia is dressed like a real princess, with a fascinator on her head and an elegant dress which ends at her mid knees. She looked no less than a member from a Duchess's family. Candy is yelling her lungs out over her father Jeffery. Roger notices Candy's high spirit and in order to start the conversation, he starts cheering with her. Candy looks at him, and he doesn't waste a second in picking the conversation. "Mr. Atkins is one of my favorite Golf Player", he says with a smile. Candy looked at him, top to toe, "Well, he is not a national level player, and how did he become your favorite?" asks Candy with a playful suspicion. Roger has an acute smile, "I am your father's... it's a POT! Did you just see that?". Roger is changing the conversation. Candy responds, "Oh yeah! That was a brilliant shot played by my dad! Ahh, you were saying something..." Roger, a tad bit nervous, "Hmm. Don't mind me saying this, but you look beautiful... do you know how to play golf?" Candy blushes, "Well, not as good as my father, but looks like I should become a member and learn how to play golf now. Do you know any good instructor? Dad won't be able to pull out time so often" Candy asks with a quirky smile. "Allow me the honor of teaching you how to play", Roger exclaims with a flirtatious look into Candy's eyes. "Oh! So you are the instructor here", replies Candy. Roger, in a calm tone, "Well, you can say that I do everything here. I am a fan of golf and enjoy volunteering myself for this sport". Candy seems impressed, "Ah, interesting! Let me introduce you with a friend of mine, Julia babe. Meet Roger. He is my golf instructor". Julia looks surprised "oh, ok, I see! Hey nice to meet you. And might I must say that was quick", Julia whispers to Candy. "So you are alone here or you are with family and friends?", asked Julia. "Yes I am with my friend, who was sitting right next to me . I think he has gone to grab something to drink. May I join you till then?" asks Roger like a polite gentleman. "Sure", responds Julia.

Meanwhile, the match gets over. Mr. Theodore is the man of the match. Julia rushes towards her father and congratulates him on winning. Mr. Theodore have his friends from work, who met Julia for the very first time at the club, took her on a walk to converse. Meanwhile, Jack joins Roger & Candy. "Hey Jack meet Candy. Candy, this is my friend Jack", Roger introduces Jack to Candy. Candy , in a nonchalant manner, "Hey!". Jack acknowledges, "Hi Candy, nice to meet you." Candy suddenly remembers "Jack, did you perform at the Edinburgh Festival? Jack, looking surprised, "Yes. I performed with my band. "Yes. The Electric Bass Orchestra–EBO!" Jack is impressed, "Oh yes. You got it right". Candy is elated, "I loved your performance. It was mind-blowing". –"Ok! Am I missing out on something or do you guys know each other already?", asks a confused Roger. Candy smiles, "Yes. Well, sort of. He performed in the festival. I was there in the audience". "That's amazing, a small world, huh?!", says Roger. Candy is jubilant "Hey Jack, let me introduce you to my best friend. I have been talking a lot about your performance to her. Jack is happy to oblige, "Sure!" But Roger interrupts "Ah, Candy he need to go. Jack has some work. He will see you again. It's really important!" Roger gives a stern look to Jack. Candy seems sad "Hey come on guys. It won't take any time. Let me introduce your celebrity friend to my best friend". Candy immediately walked off to fetch Julia from the group of oldies. Roger held Jack's hand and takes him out of the club, explaining that he approached Candy first. "Dude, you need to keep out of my way. I am trying to impress Candy. She looks so impressed with you already. This is not happening. You make distance with her", Roger said, almost demanded. Jack smiled and replies, "I have no interest in Candy. I was here because you invited me. You want me to leave, I'll leave. But this is not cool bro!"

Jack walks out from the club. Roger moves in towards Candy. Candy asks– "Where the hell did he go? I was looking everywhere. Julia is here I want to make her meet Jack. Where is he?" Roger replies– "Jack has some very important work. I told you he needed to rush. Candy is disappointed, "Oh! That's bad. I so wanted him to meet Julia.– "It is ok. May be next time I'll meet your crush", replies Julia with a wink to Candy. Roger is on the defensive "What? Crush already?!" Candy responds, blushingly, "Well yes. Sort of. He is cute", –"Ok people. Let's pack up. Candy, are you coming with me?" asks Julia. –"Well, I'll come with dad. You carry on babe. Thanks for asking", replies Candy. Roger, sheepishly, "So would you care for a coffee?" Candy "I don't mind", Candy was happy to oblige. Candy and Roger spent the rest of the evening talking over coffee and cake.

On her way back to Edinburgh, Julia's car breaks down. It's raining heavily as you can never trust the weather in Scotland. Jack is on his Bullet motorcycle. He slows down to make a call from a tele-booth nearby. He is soaked. He drops a coin and dials to his little brother, informing him that he will get late due to bad weather. As he waits for the call to be answered, he notices a BMW standing still with parking lights on, at a distance of 100 meters. There are few children playing in the rain. Suddenly, the door of the backseat of the car opens and a beautiful set of uncovered half legs come out. The heels were removed carefully from her feet. A girl comes out, walking slowly in the rain towards kids, and with a flash of light on her face, she starts dancing with those kids on the road. Jack is amused and thrilled to see this. It's the same girl he has been looking for. He is lost while looking at her. His brother is on the phone, but he is so lost that he forgets to answer him back. Suddenly, the driver calls for Julia, her car is fixed now and she leaves after saying bye to those kids. Jack is so lost that he makes no attempt of running towards her. He is just too happy to see her again and admire the other side of the girl in her. A girl who loves to dance in the rain. That moment was very special for him. He fell head over heels in love with her and to him, it is confirmed that this is truly love at first sight.

# Julia is Spellbound

As they say, time flies. Candy and Roger were dating each other, and Candy's business "The Velvet Box" was also doing very well. Julia and Candy received the project of planning the wedding for Mr. Henry Charles–one of the biggest business tycoons in New York City. After the initial consultation with Mr. Charles, they began preparations for the ground work. Candy as the day coordinator would look over the contracts with each vendor the client had chosen to hire. Wedding was to be held at The Crescent Beach Club, New York, in three weeks. Candy and Julia became extremely busy with no time to eat, drink and sleep. Working day and night on the decoration, styling, gifting, stay for the guest, music, liquor, food and so forth.

The Wedding Venue i.e. "The Crescent Beach Club" is the perfect choice by the host. Mr. Charles' own private beach awaits his guests, as the palm trees and tall beach grass sway in the gentle breeze. A perfect wedding venue, right at Long Island. Julia is totally taken aback by the location. She can't wait for the big day to come. Meanwhile, all the planning and organizing took a lot of time and now there is only a week left for the wedding. Julia and Candy had a final meet with the host, sharing all the planning and engineering done so far. Mr. Charles was quite happy with the demo look of the wedding. Perhaps he made a special yet unconventional request. His wife to be is very fond of the rock band "Aerosmith". He wants a live music show by the band as a surprise present for her at the beginning of the big fat New York wedding. Candy and Julia looked at each other, as there was no time left for them to fulfill this. But they couldn't say, no. "Sir we will check the availability of the band", politely replied Candy. They head back to their respective work location.

Julia is upset. She knows it's not possible. Aerosmith?! Now?! At the last minute! We need at least a month's time to book the band. You shouldn't have agreed to this Candy. You should have said 'No' the very minute", bellows Julia. Candy, though, is calm, "Relax babe! Let me speak to their manager once. Maybe we get lucky". Candy makes a few calls and finally gets the number of the manager of the band. "Hi, I am Lucy, how may I assist you?", responds an ominous voice on the call. Candy clears her throat with unabashed confidence, "Hey Lucy, I am Candy from velvet box wedding planners We have a special guest request. We would love to have Aerosmith perform for the wedding of Mr. Charles, a leading business tycoon from New York". Lucy seems happy "Oh, that sounds good. When is the wedding? Candy, confidently, "Ah well, we are running short on time. It is next week, on 26th September". Lucy lets out a sigh, "Oh, I am sorry. Aerosmith is already booked for 26th September. You need one month's time to book the band Candy. I am afraid we won't be able to assist you". Candy changes her tone "Please Lucy. As an exception for the first and last time, if you can manage the date". –"Darling, it's not possible. Had they been not performing on 26th at a live show, I could have still manipulated the dates. It's not in my hand. We have already taken the premium for his performance on 26th September. Thanks for calling!", Lucy hangs up. Candy gives a look to Julia. "Now what?", responds Julia. Candy, dejected, "They are already booked for $26^{th}$". –"I could sense that. So what are we doing now Candy?", asks a worried Julia. Candy has her thinking hat on, "Let me think". Candy's cell phone is vibrating. It is Roger. And suddenly as she answers the call, Candy shouts "Jack". Julia is standing close and mouths that it is Roger, not Jack.. Candy gives Julia a look, "What's wrong with you? I know what his name is". Candy walks out to answer the call, "Hey babe, how is your day shaping up?", asks Roger. –"You are a savior. Where is your friend Jack these days?" asks Candy in pertinent tone. –"Jack, why you asking for him?" inquires Roger. –"Roger, I want your friend to perform in a wedding, can you please connect me with him? He is my last hope and we are running short on time", confesses Candy. –"Oh! Well sure. Let me speak to him and get back to you", replies Roger –"Do you mind sharing his number with me? Come on baby. It's absolutely professional. I have no personal interest in him" explains Candy. –"Sure I think that will be better. Please note, its #01620-885-649. Be good my naughty girl", says Roger before Candy hangs up. Candy without wasting a minute gives a call to Jack.

Jack was practicing with his band, trying to create a new tune. Trin Trin–he gets Candy's call He answers the call on the third ring. "Hi Jack Denver this side, how may I assist you?", Jack acknowledges the call. "Hi Jack, I am so glad to be in touch with you", responded Candy. "Who is this? I am afraid I can't recognize your voice", replied Jack. "Very well! Jack, It's me Candy, from Velvet Box wedding planners", responds Candy. "Hi Candy, do we know each other?", asks Jack. –"Well yes sort of. We met at the golf club sometime back, through a common friend "Roger", she reminds jack. –"Oh, long time, how may I assist you Candy?", affirms Jack. –"Jack, I am a big fan of your music. Remember, I did mention the last time too", says Candy. –"Thank you, Candy. That's really good to hear from you", says jack –"Jack I have a proposal for you", proposes Candy. –"Go on", he inquires, eager to know more. –"We are planning the wedding for Mr. Charles. He is one of the biggest business tycoons in New York. His wife is very fond of rock music, and he wants to surprise her with a live performance of a rock band at the beginning of the event. Your name just clicked me. We are ready to pay for your band and will take care of your travel, stay and food", explains Candy. –"Well, Candy that's really thoughtful of you, but I have never performed in weddings or personal events. I perform where the tickets are sold for the performance", says Jack. –"Oh! Come on Jack. It is such an amazing offer you are getting. There will be so many people from the celebrities to dignitaries who will be attending this wedding. It's a page-3 wedding and you are saying no to it. Jack, please take your time, sleep over it and then get back to me. It's a huge opportunity for you and you must make the most of it", insists Candy. –"Well ok, Candy. I'll speak to my troop and get back to you", assures jack.– "Sounds good. Please get back to me by tomorrow morning as we are not left with time. The wedding is on the 26$^{th}$ of September and I need to book your tickets and hotel too", Candy reminds in a mildly frantic tone.– "Sure!", assures Jack.

Candy moves in to her work station. Julia is on a call with the florist, trying to close her side of chores. Candy sits back with crossed fingers, hoping a yes from Jack. –"So all good with you? Did you fix the Aerosmith requirement?", asks Julia. Candy replies– "Yes!"– "That's amazing,. So they are performing on 26th?", asks Julia. –Candy, evading the obvious, "Aah yep! A surprise for you and the Charles family is in store. – "As in?", asks Julia.– "Babe, can you leave that on me? Please, I'll work it out and I will for sure. I promise Charles will love him", replies Candy in a reassuring tone.

Julia has her eyebrow raised "Ok! Looks like you are getting someone else to perform. For Charles to love him is beyond imagination. I hope he grants him the right to perform". Candy ignores the conversation and continues with her work. Julia walks out from their office answering a call from one of the vendor's.

Jack is in conversation with his band people, discussing the proposal. The band was quite positive on the proposal and they encourage Jack to go ahead with it. This was indeed a good opportunity to improve their visibility in the market. Next morning, Jack calls Candy and confirms to perform in the wedding with his band. Candy is extremely happy. She quickly get their tickets done and their rooms booked at the Crescent Beach Resort. Jack begins the practice for the wedding performance with his band. Julia and Candy are all set to receive guests, arriving from all over the world. They give everyone a warm welcome and have them escorted to their respective rooms. Jack lands with his band at the New York Airport. Candy is there to receive them. They all make themselves comfortable, when Julia informs Candy that a couple, who are friends with Mr. Charles have reached New York and are at the airport. She asked Candy to receive them and bring them to the venue with her. –But Candy's car is already full. "I can't do it. I have no space in the car. Where will I sit? I came to receive the band", informs Candy. –"I can't say no to them Candy. You book a taxi or what so ever but you have to get them along. I am also figuring out room availability for them. So please do the needful", insists Julia. Candy disconnects the phone but has a big smile on her face "Hey EBO, welcome! Jack I have guided the driver. He will take you all straight to the hotel. This is your room key. Its 601 & 602. Make yourself comfortable. I'll do another pickup and see you guys soon at the venue. For anything else, I am just a call away", announces Candy. Jack smiles. He took the keys and moved towards the hotel.

The band reaches the hotel, Julia is standing there with stewards to offer welcome drinks to the guests. Jack walk towards the resort, heading slowly towards Julia. She is standing and smiling from a distance towards guests coming in. That very minute, Jack comes into her sight. But she gets a call from Candy and she turns the other side to speak to her. Jack is standing right behind her, dressed in a white T, black denim jeans and Ray Ban Wayfarer sunglasses. He smiles at everyone and takes his welcome drink. He heads towards the lobby for the check-in formalities. Julia is on the call,"Candy, please hurry up and reach soon. We need to start with the lunch in sometime".

It was this close that Jack and Julia missed seeing each other face to face. Jack, without wasting a minute, takes a round of the wedding venue and observes where they have to perform. Standing close to the stage where the performance is to take place, Jack does some calculations at the podium. Julia walks by and finds him standing alone. She assumes he is a guest at the wedding. She walk towards him and on a polite note, asks him "Hi Sir, are you looking for something?" Jack turns back and here he is right in front of the woman he has been looking for everywhere. Jack is speechless for a moment. Julia asks him again, "Sir, is all good with you? Do need anything?" Jack smiles and says, "I just got everything". Immediately there is buzz on her phone and Julia is informed "The host is there with the guest of honor. We have to start the lunch. Please come!". Julia smiles at Jack and invites him for the lunch. She quickly leaves. Jack looks up and then looks down with a smile. He whispers her name "Julia", followed by "I am coming".

The lunch is being served and all the guests are very happy and comfortable. They are thankful to the Velvet Box for this warm welcome and of course to Mr. Charles for getting the best wedding planners who know what best suits them. Julia walks to Candy and asks her "what next?" Lunch is almost done. By evening, "Your band has to perform. Have you informed Mr. Charles about this?" Julia asked with stress. Candy says, "Ok babe! Let's speak to him now. He looks like he is in a good mood". Candy walks towards Mr. Charles and says "Sir, please can we a buy a minute of yours?". Mr. Charles excuses himself from the guests and head towards the conference room with Candy and Julia.

Candy informs him, without wasting a minute, "Sir, we regret to inform that Aerosmith is not available for the performance due to some reason. However, we have organized a very good rock band performance." Mr. Charles is taken aback, "What are you saying? Almost everyone knows Aerosmith is performing live before the ceremony." Julia chuckles between the two. Her stress level is increasing. –"Sir, trust me. I have seen them perform. They are really good and as much as I know how important this day is for you, I will make sure you enjoy every bit of it. And what really matters is that you are there with ma'am, for her today. It's you who is the most special person, not a band", Candy explains with stellar confidence. Mr. Charles smiles at Candy and says "You are really good, you know that? Ok girls, do whatever you feel is best, as I have no choice. I can't change the wedding planner's last minute." Mr. Charles laughs and walks out. Julia looks at Candy, "When did you get time to perform so much in front of him?" They share a hearty laugh. "By the way who is performing?", asks Julia. –"Remember the band EBO?", asks Candy. Julia tries to remember, "Entertainment box office?" –"No darling. It's The Electronic Bass Orchestra. The band that performed at the festival of Edinburgh, which you missed watching. Does something click you now? Julia remembers, "Oh my God! I hope they are good enough. Babe, you should have got a celebrity band. No one knows him and this is going to be a big mess". Candy calmly replies, "That's exactly why I didn't tell you anything! You need to calm down and trust my decision now".

Candy & Julia move towards the beach where the ceremony is to take place. They are checking on the decoration and displays. As the sun sets, guests start pouring in at the wedding point. They are escorted towards their respective seats for the band's performance which is scheduled to start in the next few minutes. Jack organizes the systems, checks on the mic and his guitar. His band members all settle on the stage. Julia escorts the maid of honor to the venue and makes a small announcement. They introduce the band "Hi all. We are here to bless the beautiful couple Edward Charles and Catherine Hamilton. But before we proceed with the wedding vows, I would like to introduce a small surprise organized for Catherine by Charles. Presenting a performance by THE EBO! People are excited. Catherine smiles at Edward with an "Awwwwww look". EBO is all set to present their top hits from the old school. Jack gets the spotlight on him and he starts singing while playing his magical guitar. Julia is love struck. She can't believe her eyes. It's the man she met few hours back and she was not aware he is the main guitarist and singer from the band. Each note of his guitar seemed to hit Julia's heart. She couldn't stop moving her body to his electrifying performance. She keeps looking at him perform, and finally the moment comes when Jack and Julia both have an alluring eye contact with each other. This one Jack plays just for her, "She can kill with her smile, she can wound with her eyes, she can ruin your faith with her casual lies and she only reveals, what she wants you to see, she hides like a child but she's always a woman to me". With a sweet end to the performance, Jack receives a huge round of applaud. "Come on people! Let's clap from both the hands", Candy shouted rallying for a louder applause. "Yes EBO! This was an amazing experience. Edward, thank you baby, I love you for this. Amazing. These guys are too good", exclaimed Catherine. Mr. Charles looked at Candy and Julia, and with a happy nod expressed his gratitude for this incredible performance.

# Jack & Julia

Everyone loved the show. The wedding takes place and the priest is there to address the groom and bride. Charles and Catherine begin taking their wedding vows. Catherine says "I do!" Julia is lost in the vows, admiring the couple and this moment. Jack makes a move, afraid he will be missing out on the opportunity again. He goes up to Julia and stands right next to her. He whispers, "Beautiful". Julia looks at him. He completes, "..isn't this the most beautiful feeling in the world". Julia smiles and says, "Indeed Mr... ?" He whispers again with a little more bend, "Jack, but my friends call me JD with love". Julia had a broad smile, "JD? Jack Daniel, like seriously?" Jack responds, "Jack Denver", with a smile. Jack asks her, "May I have the honor of taking you for a walk Ms. Julia?" He asked with a twinkle in his eyes. Julia blushes and replies with the attitude to make it clear that she is in no hurry, "Well, the wedding vows are still on. And I am the wedding planner here. I need to organize the other half of the wedding event. I doubt I can pull out time for a walk with you Mr. Denver. Perhaps I really want to congratulate you for such an amazing performance. I enjoyed a lot. You are really good." She smiles, looks forward and takes a small step ahead, to show that her attention really is in the ceremony. Jack whispers, "I'll be waiting for you, at the beach, Ms wedding planner". He slowly disappears.

Julia's heart is beating like never before. The mature woman in her is moved by Jack's approach. This is the very first time for her. Is it an attraction or the strongest feeling of love at first sight? Julia is lost in her own thoughts when Candy reaches out to her and shakes her in standing position, bringing her back to the real world. "Julia babes are you here?", questioned Candy. –"Of course! Yes, we need to get ready with drinks and dinner. It's time. The guests will head towards the dining arrangements, right after the vows", Julia responds with a shaky confidence. "Hmmm, that's exactly what I came to say. Perhaps before that I want to know how did you find the performance?", asks Candy. –"It was good, Candy. You are a life saver. I won't doubt on you next time", remarks Julia. "Well, well, well! I know, I know I am the best", Candy comments, celebrating herself. She moves away to make a call to Roger. "Hey Roger, your friend just killed it. What an amazing performance. He saved my job, like literally", she exclaims. –"I am glad. Where is he? Is he there?", asks Roger. –"Yes! Where will he go? He is Charles special guest now. He has impressed the dignitaries big time. And…", Candy continues to shower praise on Jack.

Julia, on the other hand, is thinking whether she should go and see him at the beach or show him the attitude. Julia often speaks to herself when she is in double mind. She looked at herself in the mirror and asked, "Do you think it will be too desperate for me to go and see him? I barely know him." She questions herself. Then, she smiles and replies to herself, "Well he has invited you so gracefully. He finds honor in taking you out on a walk. You must be nice to him and not make him wait more. She smiles big to herself and combs her hair. She gives a little touch up to herself and quickly hurtles towards the beach.

Jack was looking at the full moon, waiting for his lady love. He is standing at peace with himself. Julia joins him, "Mr. Denver, please don't think I am here to accompany you. The moon looked interesting to me. I thought of joining you in the watch". Jack looks at her from top to toe. He takes a deep breath and takes out his hand from his trouser pocket, stretching it out in her direction. Julia holds his hand, goes closer. They greet each other. –"Hi", Julia greets him. –"Thank you for coming", Jack replies. Both start walking bare feet at a slow pace. –"I have been looking for you since long. Do you know that?", says Jack. "Looking for me? Really? No, I don't know that", is the honest response from Julia. –"I saw this beautiful girl sipping her cappuccino while reading a book at the lake side. She was top to toe dressed no less than a celebrity. The second time I saw you was at Edinburgh festival main event. I performed there last year. I saw you, sitting right in the front row with the audience. I tried to reach you but you left. The third time I saw you in North Berwick. You came out from a BMW which was down for some reason. You danced in the rain with those kids on the road. A flash of light came on your face and I completely lost myself to you", Jack fondly remembers and recounts for Julia. Julia is thrilled and speechless, she says, fumbling a bit, "a...a a a I am speechless. That's interesting, Mr. Denver. I must say you have been literally looking for me. What if I wouldn't have met you?", ponders Julia. –"Hmmm. Thats not possible. With so much desire I craved you, that the entire universe conspired to make this meeting possible. We were destined to meet, and here I am right in front of you", Jack replies with a charm in his tone. Julia is smiling, "So what do you do Mr. Denver, other than flattering women?" Jack chuckles "Did I flatter you? Well, well, well, genuine feelings have to go through a hell of a struggle. But back to your basic question, Ms. Julia, I am a guitarist and a singer for my band, the EBO, which just became popular because of your wedding planner partner. Ms Candy's believe in us".

"Oh my god you two, what are you doing here? Thanks Jack, but you deserved it and more to go", Candy surprises the two of them. The three laugh. –"Jack, I need to take my friend from you, if you don't mind", says Candy. –"And if

I do?", Jack asks. –"Well, then you can join her back for dinner. We need to organize and wrap up a few things", informs Candy. –"Just kidding. Please go ahead", Jack responds. Jack looked at Julia with a smile of seeing her back in sometime. Julia blushes and walks away with Candy.

Candy and Julia were on their way. "So Jack was the guitarist I was talking about. Remember, when you missed his performance. Small world yeah?", says Candy. Julia smiles and keeps walking. –"Ok! We need to talk", Candy suggests. "Let's finish this wedding and we shall", replies Julia.

Julia and Candy are at the dinner table, raising a toast for the most adorable couple, Mr. & Mrs. Charles, "Heres to the newly weds. Yeahhh!!! Everyone dinner will be served now". Mrs. Charles asks Candy and Julia to invite Jack for dinner with them. Candy runs to fetch Jack. Candy and Jack walk towards Mrs. Charles dinner table. –"May I have the honor of joining you Mrs. Charles?", Jack asks with a smile. –"Of course Jack! That goes without asking. You made our wedding so special with your performance. I believe even Aerosmith wouldn't have been so good", comments the newly wed Mrs. Charles. Mr. Charles was surprised and happy to hear that. –"I am honored Ma'am. I am glad we could perform to that level", responds Jack in a humble tone. Mr. Charles turns to Jack, "Jack, what will you have wine or whiskey?" Jack promptly responds "With dinner, I take wine Sir. Mr. Charles smiles and instructs a waiter to show him the red and white option. Jack says, "Red". –"You are just like one of us Jack. Even I am fond of red wine. Let me offer you my favorite from the collection", remarks the newly wed groom. Mr. Charles claps his hands and shouts "Attendant, please serve my guest Chateau Lafite 1787. Jack, it is the most expensive standard bottle of wine. This vintage is believed to be from Thomas Jefferson's cellar", Mr. Charles smiles and gives warm cheers to Jack. Jack acknowledges the conversation and shows his gratitude with a "Thank you".

Dinner is over. Everyone is moving out, heading towards their rooms. It's been a long day. Candy and Julia make the payment to the vendors. Jack calls Candy and asks her to connect him with Julia. Candy gives him Julia's number. Jack makes her the first call however nervously disconnects the call. He makes a second call. This time he holds his nerve. She answers the phone, "Hi this is Julia Theodore, and how may I assist you?" "Hi Ms. Theodore, is this the right time to speak to you?", jokes Jack. –"Well, depends what you want to talk about Mr. Denver", asks Julia, playing along. "I wanted to ask you, what is your plan? Where are you heading tomorrow? As the wedding is over now", enquires Jack. "Hmmm, good question. My father called. He has a match in NBGC.

So I'll be taking a flight to North Berwick", she says. "What a coincidence! I am flying to North Berwick too. You know, I live there. What time is your flight, if I may ask? "You ask too much", is Julia's playful response. "Hmmm I know but I am just so curious to know everything about you", is Jack's playful retort Julia blushes, "I am taking United Airlines, departing day after at 7:50am. It's a non–stop flight. And before you ask me. It is a 6hr 55 minutes flight. Jack laughs, "You are cute, I am glad it's a non–stop flight and I am even glad that we have the whole day tomorrow to ourselves". "Who said I am free. I have lot of work and I need to pack", Julia is stern. "Hmmm, means you are absolutely free. I'll wait for you at Bond 45 NY. "Ah. You never give up", sighs Julia. "Never ever! See you beautiful, sleep tight", Jack waits for Julia to hang up. Julia smiles and hangs up! Candy walks down to Julia's room, "All packed babe?", she asks. "Yeah, most of it", Julia replies. "We have an early morning. You please set an alarm", instructs Candy. "Babe I am sorry I forgot to inform you. I am leaving day after. Dad has a match. So I have rescheduled my flight from Edinburgh to North Berwick. "Are you for real? When did you do that? You should have told me. I would have come with you. Would have met Roger too. Hey hang on! I hope it's just the match or are you trying to hide something from me?", asks an inquisitive Candy. "You need to take a chill pill babe. Nothing as such", says Julia, easing Candy's suspicion. "Jack is flying day after too. What is going on? Come on, I am your best friend", Candy is relentless. "Babe I told you dad has a match and that is it", reaffirms Julia. "Ok! See you soon. Back to work in Edinburgh. Keep me posted about your landing", Candy finally eased her curiosity. They both hugged and wished each other goodnight. Candy walked back to her room.

It was a beautiful morning. Julia, the sleeping beauty, is looking her best while fast asleep. She wakes up to the sound of music. She rubs her eyes and stretches as she sits up. She looks at the window where she feels the music is coming from. She walks towards her portico, wearing an alluring wrap from the night. Her hair, long and curly, is falling on one side of her shoulder. She looks down and to her surprise Jack is standing like a real-life Romeo, playing the guitar, accompanied by a few other musicians. They were there to wishing the beautiful lady the most amazing morning of her life. Jack plays the guitar and sings for her, a song from 80's written by Steve Perry:

*'Just a small-town girl*

*Livin' in a lonely world*

*She took the midnight train goin' anywhere*

*Just a city boy*

*Born and raised in south Detroit*

*He took the midnight train goin' anywhere.*

*A singer in a smoky room.*

*A smell of wine and cheap perfume*

*For a smile they can share the night*

*It goes on and on, and on, and on*

*Strangers waiting*
*Up and down the boulevard*
*Their shadows searching in the night*
*Streetlights, people*
*Living just to find emotion*
*Hiding somewhere in the night*
*Working hard to get my fill*
*Everybody wants a thrill*
*Payin' anything to roll the dice*
*Just one more time*
*Some will win, some will lose*
*Some were born to sing the blues*
*Oh, the movie never ends*
*It goes on and on, and on, and on*
*Strangers waiting*
*Up and down the boulevard*
*Their shadows searching in the night*
*Streetlights, people*
*Living just to find emotion*
*Hiding somewhere in the night*
*Don't stop believin'*
*Hold on to the feelin'*
*Streetlights, people*

*Don't stop believin'*

*Hold on*

*Streetlights, people*

*Don't stop believin'*

*Hold on to the feelin'*

*Streetlights, people"*

Julia can't stop smiling. She rushes down to the veranda, where Jack was playing and singing with other musicians. "Yeaaahh! You are too good, man", comments one of the guests. Julia contains her excitement and walks like a lady towards Jack. She looks into his eyes. He is still, lost in her gaze. Jack whispers, "Am I privileged for a kiss or am I allowed to take a kiss?" Jack asks Julia this question, with a feverous passion in his voice. Julia looks at him in his eyes. She moves closer and slowly whispers, "You deserve a kiss, Mr.Rockstar". She makes the first move for her first kiss. It is the most erotic kiss, ever witnessed by the hotel guests and staff.

Their eyes are closed and they are totally lost in each other, unaware of the crowd around. During this salacious moment, one of the guests takes their perfect picture. Julia takes a step back, releasing Jack from her arm. She finally gets a hold of herself, realising the people around. She assesses her dressing and the situation. She pulls herself back, smiling at Jack and walks swiftly to her room. She closes the bedroom door, taking a deep breath. She looks at herself in the mirror and admires herself. To herself, she says "What a feeling, Jack! Seriously! I literally kissed him.

On the other hand, Jack is waving at everyone. What a heroic moment! The oldie who clicked their picture, walked towards Jack and gave him a friendly gesture, "Here young boy. I believe it's your first kiss. Here is your trophy. Cherish this forever." Jackthanks the old timer, "Thank you sir. That's really thoughtful of you". "The best click of my life", the old man jokes. Jack keeps the picture in his wallet. Heading towards the lobby, he calls Julia and reminds her of the breakfast waiting at Bond 45. "Yes, just give me 10 minutes. I'll quickly take shower and join you", she tells him. "Take your time. I have arranged the car for you and just call for 011786. Your chauffeur will get the car from the valley", informs Jack.

Julia gets ready. She had adorned herself in an exclusive Pink Prada dress, paired with white Louboutin, light makeup for the day and few accessories, a watch and earrings. Julia locks her room, reaches out to the reception at the lobby and asks the executive to call her chauffeur 011786. She waits at the lounge, when one of the executive informs about the chauffeur's arrival. Julia walks towards the car. The chauffeur open the back door of the car. While greeting her, he says, "Good Day Ma'am. Will you be comfortable at the backseat or you would want to experience the drive on the front seat with Me?" Julia is surprised by what she just heard. She looks up while speaking, "How dare you!..." And to her ultimate thrill, its Jack. "What the hell! Really?! So you are the chauffeur", said Julia, with a happy face. "So want to join this chauffeur at the front seat?", Jack asked again. Julia closes the back seat door of the car with a smooth jerk by her haunch, takes the front seat. Jack plays some soft music, heading for their first breakfast date. Jack compliments Julia, "You look great as always". Julia retorts "You too look good in this chauffeur uniform". Jack laughs, "Haha. Different, isn't it?" – "I don't know what to say but it's cute and fun", she says with a gentle laugh.

They reach Bond 45. Jack talks about the place. Bond 45 is best known for its vegetable antipasto bar which offers a rotating selection of market vegetables and features an expansive menu that includes specialty veal chops, seafood, house made pasta, thin crust pizza and breakfast all day. Jack pulls the chair for Julia, like a real gentleman, making her as comfortable as possible. He asks the attendant to give the menu card to the lady. She shall order for them. Julia looks at the card, and like any other girl, she is too confused to place an order. She passes the card to Jack saying, "Well you decided the place, now you decide the order". Jack is perplexed but prepared, "Ah is it? Ok, let me order a finger licking meal for you.. Instantly, Julia speaks "Please order light. I don't really eat much in the morning". Jack gives an order for avocado toast and poached eggs and blueberry buttermilk french toast, along with a cappuccino and a double espresso. Attendant looked at Julia to confirm, "Anything else Ma'am? "That's all", responds Julia. Jack, looking at Julia, asks, "You love wearing brands!?" "Yes, they are so exclusive. Don't you like brands?" "No, not like to the extent you do I have no time or money to invest in such brands", Jack responds in all honesty. "Its the stories and experience one spends on", Julia sounds poetic. "Oh really! I thought it is the quality and craftsmanship one spends on", Jack responds with a bit of irritation. "That goes without saying", Julia responds calmly. "What's your favourite brand?", Jack asks, pulling his chair a bit closer. "If you don't have time and money to invest on such brands, what's the point of knowing?", Julia asks, expecting another intelligent answer. "Well, not for myself, but maybe someday for you, when I can afford it", Jack satisfies Julia's expectation with his answer. Julia is smiling but she doesn't want to give herself away again. She responds calmly "I will tell you, when that time is nearer." Attendant serves the breakfast. They both enjoy their morning brunch.

"Can I have the cheque please?", Jack asks as they prepare to leave. The attendant brings the bill. Jack makes the payment. They leave. While on the way, Jack tells Julia about his family and career. Jack has no one in his family other than a little brother, who goes to school, studying in nursery. At present, his brother is staying with his beloved uncle and aunt, who takes care of them like their own children. Julia talks about her father. "Hmm so you are William Theodore's daughter", he looks at her and smiles. Jack driving and thinking about the huge family background difference between the two. Julia asks him to stop the car. There was a beautiful church on their way to hotel. She stops to make a visit and offer a prayer for a while. Jack, looking at her innocent face, he realizes he is very much in love with her. He sat beside her and asked his lord, "Oh Lord please give her whatever she has asked." When Julia opens her eyes, she looks at him. They smile at each other and head towards the hotel. As they reach the hotel, Julia quickly collects her luggage and so does Jack. They checkout and head towards the airport. Jack and Julia are at the airport. They clear the check-in formalities and head towards boarding. "So I'll see you when we land now", Jack says, dreading the separation. "Hmmm". Julia responds. She realised she is sitting in business class and Jack's seat is in economy. Boarding starts. They call for business passengers first. Julia kisses him and boards her flight. Jack boards later as they start the boarding for economy passengers.

While the plane starts taxing on the runway, Julia is thinking, it's a seven hours flight. He is here and I am not with him. She immediately asks the airhostess, "Dear, you have a passenger Jack Denver flying economy. Can you please check if you can upgrade him to business. I see very few business flyers in the flight". The airhostess says, "Ma'am, I have to check with the pilot. Its a connecting flight. We will have passengers from

North Berwick to Edinburgh". Julia, smiles and says, "He is flying to North Berwick." Airhostess smiles and replies, "I'll check ma'am." The airhostess gets the approval from the pilot. She informs Julia and goes to Jack, "Mr. Denver, we have a guest in business who is willing to upgrade your seat, will you be comfortable with that?" He smiles and says, "I would love to." Jack gets a seat close to Julia and they are together again. "Welcome on board", says Julia. "Well thanks for upgrading me. You couldn't handle 15 minutes without me, could you?", he jokes. "Well, there were a lot of empty seats. So I thought of calling you. Don't get any ideas", she smiled and looked out of the window. The plane takes off, Jack held her hand in flight. It feels so good, when you have that someone who hold your hand. She sensed a security, care and lot of love. They were different from any regular couple. They didn't ask each other about their past life. Jack was a practical man, who believed in the present and making that beautiful. At present, he was the only reality to Julia and he was quite aware of it.

They land. They walk down holding hands. There is a silence between the two. "This is so unexpected. I never thought I would.., like you know what I mean. Life looks so changed", comments Julia. "Yes, I know what you mean. Even I am quite thrilled with this. I was sure I will meet you but will I hold your hand and fly to North Berwick? Not so soon", Jack confesses. "Hey join me for the golf match. I'll make you meet father", Julia suggests. "Sure I would love to meet him. let me go home and see my little brother. I will call you", he ascents. He escorts her till the car. She leaves and he calls a taxi for himself.

Jack's little brother John, is extremely happy at seeing Jack home. They hug each other and spend some quality time with each other. Jack shares his performance video with him. John is super excited seeing brother perform. Jack's uncle and aunt, who are taking care of John, also encourage Jack for his career. They are very happy to see him grow. Like parents, they shower their blessings on both, Jack and John.

Julia's father is happy to see her. He takes her out on lunch and they have the best father daughter time. Mr. Theodore looks at Julia and informs her, "There is a special guest, attending the match." "Well, even I have a special friend coming over to watch your game father. "A special friend? Ok that's interesting. Did you meet him at Mr. Charles wedding?", inquires her curious father. "Yes father, you will be happy to see him", Julia smiles and responds. Mr. Theodore closes the conversation about the special guest he mentioned. They relax for a while and head towards the golf club.

People start pouring in, one after the other. Mr. Theodore's special guest is here too. Caledon Hockley, an Argentine hotelier and real estate developer, who has developed properties in his native Buenos Aires, as well as Miami Beach, Florida. Caledon is the founder and President of the Hockley Group. He is one of the youngest achievers in his industry. Mr. Theodore welcomes Caledon. "I am so glad to have you here Cal", Mr Theodore said. "It's my honour", replied Caledon. While the match is about to begin, Julia is waiting for Jack. She keeps looking at the entrance of the club. Mr. Theodore calls Julia, "Julia, remember I told you about a special guest. Meet Caledon. He is my special man today. Cal, Julia is my only daughter. She will take care of you, while I am getting ready for the match". Caledon replies, "Don't worry sir. You please get ready, I can't wait for the match to begin". "I will see you both in a while", Mr. Theodore says as he leaves to prepare for his match. Caledon looks at Julia. She looks distracted, "Is there something that's bothering you Ms. Julia?", Caledon asks. "No. I was expecting a friend of mine. He is not here yet", she says without really making eye contact. Caledon responds, "Oh! I see. Why don't you call him and check?" Julia looks at him and replies, "Thank you. I think I should ask now. Its high time. Please excuse me, Caledon". Julia leaves him to call Jack, but her father Theodore calls her back. Mr. Theodore is trying his level best for both to click with each other.

# Jack's Dilemma

Julia is calling Jack. He isn't answering the call. She is upset. She goes back and stands with Caledon.

The match begins. Caledon is looking at Julia, hoping to catch her looking at him. He finds her pretty. He initiates the conversation, "So Julia looks like your friend isn't here and this has made you really upset". "No. Nothing such. Anyway, so what do you do Caledon? Looks like father is really fond of you", asks Julia. 'Well, you can call me Cal. I am a hotelier and your father is partnering with me in an upcoming project", Caledon replies with the calm of an industrialist. "Oh! That sounds interesting", Julia responds. Mr. Theodore notices Julia and Cal in conversation. It is exactly what he wanted.

The match is over. He joins the two. Mr. Theodore lost the match. "You played well sir. I am sorry to see you lose." Mr. Theodore replies, "Well you have no idea what I have won", and he laughs loudly. He looks at Julia and says, "Daughter, Mr. Caledon is our guest here. I want you to take him around, show him the city. He has never traveled this side of the country." Julia smiles "Well, I am not aware much about North Berwick, but I will make sure we get to see the place" and she excuses herself. Julia returns to the hotel. Jack calls her 7-8 times. She has not answered a single call. Julia changes to her night dress. Jack goes to the hotel reception and asks for her. The receptionist connects the call. Julia answers the phone "Yes!" "Ms. Julia, we have a guest who would like to speak to you", informs the receptionist. She passes the phone to Jack, "I am sorry my love. Please allow me a chance to explain myself." Julia is angry and she hangs up without a reply. Jack is in no mood to give up. He looks at the receptionist and pretends that the guest has asked him to come over. He requests her to ask someone to escort him to her room. The lady at the reception calls one of the attendants and asks him to escort him to room 712.

On the way, someone calls the attendant for another work. He guides Jack with the directions to room 712. Jack walks with a smile toward his lady love's room. He picks a rose from one of the centre table.

Julia is upset and is trying her best to sleep. There is a knock on the door. She shouts, "Who is it?!" On getting no reply, she walks to the door and slowly opens it. A rose pops in first. She opens the door and it is Jack. She tries to close the door on his face, but he stops with his hand and says, "That's how you welcome people at your door?" She turns around with an upset face and allows him to get in. He closes the door and stands right behind her. He held her from behind seeking an apology. She turns towards him, not ready to look in his eyes. He whispers "I am sorry. John was not well. I had to stay back with him." Julia looks at him slowly, "What happened? You should have informed me." "Well, I tried to but I guess I managed now", he says. "Father lost the match. I also told him about you. I said there is a special guest coming over. And then he made me meet his special guest, Caledon. I have to show him around. Hey why don't you join us tomorrow?", she asks, excited. "Who is he?", Jack asks. Julia explains, "He is a business partner with father in his upcoming venture. Father wants me to show him around". Jack thinks for a moment, "I doubt I can join you, but I'll let you know where you can take him". "That is so thoughtful of you. Where are you so busy that you can't join us?", she asks, with genuine concern. "I have some auditions and practice sessions with my band", he answers. "Ok", she says holding his hand. Jack holds her and says, "Make yourself free soon from Caledon and I'll see you". Julia and Jack smile and kiss each other goodnight. Jack leaves the room like a gentleman.

Jack couldn't sleep the whole night, Caledon's introduction by Mr. Theodore to Julia was more than a business partnership. He decides to not let Julia be alone in the city. He reaches Hotel early morning, knocks on the lady's door and says, "Room service". Julia getting ready, is talking to herself, "Room service? Did I order anything?"

She quickly wears her bathing gown and climbs out of the bathtub. And a pleasant surprise. Julia smiles and says, "Jack did you just take this job?". They share a laugh together. Jack walks in closes the door "So madam, would you care for tea, coffee or a hot kiss?" "Well, I don't mind a coffee with a hot shower", replies Julia. She removes her bathing gown. Jack can't hold himself anymore. He walk towards her held her tight and they make love to each other for the first time. He can't stop kissing her and she can't resist his hard bare chest on her naked wet body. They rubbed their torsos against each other. Finally, they landed in the shower together. Jack says "You know what. I was in-secure. I can't leave you alone with anyone so random". "I thought so. Are you joining us?", she asks "Yes I am joining you but as a guide. He should not know me. You are not introducing us", Jack says so with a sternness. Julia laughs, "Thats funny why would you not want to get introduced", she questions playfully. –"I haven't met your father yet. Let me first meet him and then you can introduce me", he suggests. Julia nods, "I got you". Jack smiles, "You are a smart girl".

They get ready. "I am waiting in the lobby for you", he tells her at the door. "See you in five minutes", she replies, as she gets ready. Julia calls Caledon, "Hey Caledon, a very good morning to you. Caledon, on the other side, "Hi Julia. Please call me Cal. Wish you a wonderful morning too. You sound so chirpy. Excited to take me out?"

Julia snickers, "Well, I have a special guide who will assist us to look around. "A guide? Why do we need one, we can go ourselves", Caledon sounds disappointed. "Well, Cal I normally prefer seeing a new place with a guide. They have a good idea about every place", she retorts, trying to sound convincing. "Ok! So I'll see you in the lobby", Caledon says. "I am right there, come over", Julia says before hanging up.

Julia leaves her room, Mr. Caledon has also reached. She is looking around for Jack. "You look lovely", Caledon surprises her. "Thank you!", she remarks. She takes out her phone to call Jack. There he is at the main entrance. "There he is. The guide. shall we?", she suggests. "After you", he suggests. Jack takes the back seat with Julia, Caledon is a bit aghast, "Excuse me. Do you mind sitting in front with the driver?" Jack turns his gaze to Julia "I told you, I don't appreciate being treated like a guide", Jack huffs. Julia smile wryly "I am so sorry sir. Cal, he is Mr. Hop Williams. He is not an ordinary guide. He is a very popular, well known "cicerone". He is our guest and we must respect him for taking out time to show us around", she explains. Caledon finds this funny. Without saying anything, he sits in front with the chauffeur. Jack as Mr. Hop Williams asks the chauffeur to take them to the "Buttercup Café". "We must try the hot chocolate here. They are very good", remarks Jack. Caledon is not happy"Seriously? That's the first place we stop? A café shop?" Jack calmly retorts, "It's not just a café shop. It is the Buttercup café shop. Julia jumps in "Oh! I love hot chocolate. I even missed my breakfast. Come on Cal! Let's sit here for a while".

Caledon and Julia order a cappuccino for themselves and a hot chocolate for Jack. Jack was carrying horse feed pounce in a small packet with him. He secretly pours the powder in Caledon's cappuccino and leaves it for Julia to stir. Julia is unaware of his mischief, Caledon takes the first sip of his coffee. He quite liked the Vanilla flavor and he enjoys having cappuccino. They push off from the café. Jack sits back with Julia and Caledon sits in front. Caledon asks "So where are we heading now Mr. William? Jack says "We will now head towards the Scottish Seabird Centre". Caledon likes this suggestion better, "A seabird centre. Oh ok. But I am not much of a wildlife person though. Julia jumps in again,"This will be so much fun. I have always yearned for birds, and they are so beautiful". Jack looks at Julia and sighs. Meanwhile Caledon feels a rise of uncomfortable disturbance in his stomach, but he ignores it, thinking it will settle in sometime.

They reach the seabird centre. Julia can't stop admiring the wild life. Wild yet beautiful and so innocent. Caledon walks towards Julia and says, "Yes it is a good place. They have kept a variety of species here, quite interesting". Jack finds a cameraman and asks them to join in for a picture. While standing close to make a pose, Caledon could feel a lot of uneasiness, which was growing stronger. He excuses himself and rushes towards the washroom. Julia inquires "Are you alright Cal? Caledon says, as he rushes to the restroom, "Allow me sometime. I will join you right away". Jack says loudly "Come on Caledon, we are getting a picture clicked". Jack is turning as nasty as he can with Caledon. However, Caledon excuses himself and rushes to the washroom. Jack gives a nasty smile. Julia notices him. Julia asks, "What is it? You are wearing a nasty look". Jack is grinning, "Well I was a naughty child. Julia gets it "I believe you. So what have you done? Naughty boy! Jack smirks, "I did nothing. Looks like Cappuccino didn't suit your Cal. The cameraman is holding the camera "Sir, madam are you ready for the picture? Jack pulls Julia close, always ready. Caledon is all exhausted walks terribly towards Julia, Julia asks with concern, "Cal, you ok?" Caledon replies "No, I am not I am sorry I need to go back to the Hotel". Jack arrives, "Oh God, what has happened? Is your stomach upset?" Caledon isn't very happy, "Mr. Hop Williams, excellent observation". Julia is embarrassed, "Oh Lord, allow me to call a doctor". "No, no, I will call one at the hotel. Julia you please carry on. I will take the car if you don't mind as I really need to rush", he tells her politely. "Please do. We will take a taxi", says Julia. "I am sure Mr. William will have friends as a cab driver, who can assist you well", Caledon says before he leaves. Jack smiles, "Yes. Don't worry. I'll take care of her. You please take care of yourself". Caledon holds his stomach and tries to walk as fast as he can. Julia looks at Jack and says, "Why do I have a feeling that you have done something?" Jack laughs, "Not me. Mr. Hop Williams. "How convenient! What did you do? Please tell me", Jack prods. "Ok! I just added horse feed pounce in his cappuccino, which you stirred assuming its sugar", confesses Jack. "What? You can't be serious, Oh my God. You are too much, Jack. That is so bad. I hope he gets well soon", she says. "Well, the weather is beautiful. Let me show you North Berwick, my love", he smiles and says.

Jack takes Julia around. He shows her the Dirleton Castle followed by Bass Rock, North Berwick Law and the exotic sea cliff, which incorporates the scenic beach views of the Bass Rock and Tantallon Castle, as well as forest walking trails. "My eyes are so exhausted. What a beautiful city you live in Jack", Julia says. Jack goes down on his knees, "Will you be happy to live your whole life with me here?" He is asking with his hand towards her. Julia is shocked, "Are you proposing?" "What else does it look like?", he remarks. "Well, I'll think over it and let you know", she says, trying to escape the moment. "Seriously? Well I don't mind moving to Edinburgh", he says. Julia suddenly explains "No, I want to come to North Berwick, leaving all that I have behind. Yes I want to live with you now and forever". They kiss each other. "I am struggling at the moment but I have faith in my struggle. You will not regret your decision", Jack says while holding her close. "Bottom line, I love you!", she confidently confesses. Jack sings,

*"Julia, Julia, give me your answer do*
*I am half crazy all for the love of you*
*It won't be stylish a marriage*
*I can't afford a carriage*
*but you'll look sweet upon the seat*
*of a bicycle made for two"*

Julia is also overwhelmed. She smiles and sings back to him,

*"Jacky Jacky, here is my answer true*
*I am all crazy just for the love of you*
*You can blast the bloomy carriage*
*all that matters to me is our marriage*
*And I presume that I'll look like a moon*
*on your bicycle made for two"*

The laughed and hugged each other. A day well spent, Jack takes Julia home. She meets his little brother John. She plays with him. John is already so fond of Julia. Jack also introduces her to his uncle and aunt. They all enjoyed an evening together. Julia was invited to stay back for dinner. She couldn't say no. It is late and she gets a call from her father, Mr. Theodore asks, "How was your day Julia?" "Father, it was good". Mr. Theodore questions further, "Are you not at the hotel?" "No I was out for dinner at a friend's place. I am leaving for hotel in about sometime", she informs. There is a pause and then Mr. Theodore responds "I am waiting".

# The Love Confession

"I need to leave now. It's really late. It was lovely meeting you all. And John, you are a sweetheart. I'll see you soon again darling",

Julia says, while rushing out. Jack notices Julia is a little worried. He calms her and says, "Don't worry I will show up whenever you want me to. I love you baby", Jack kisses her and escorts her to the hotel. Mr. Theodore waiting at the hotel lobby He notices Jack seeing off Julia. He heads towards her room. Julia meets him in her room passage. She quickly unlocks her room. They walk inside in complete silence.

Julia speaks first, "Father, you should have told me we are meeting each other today, I would have not made so late". Mr. Theodore smiles in a meaningful manner, "Daughter, since when have we started needing appointments to see each other. It's okay, you went out with your friend. Now you are here for me. So what I really want to know is that what went wrong with Caledon, I assumed you were to take him out today". Julia proceeds to explain, "Yes Father I did. We went out but unfortunately his stomach got upset and he decided to go back to his hotel". "And you decided to stay back with your guide. The same guide who I believe just dropped you at the hotel gate", Mr. Theodore unhappiness is clear in his tone. "No, no that is my friend not a guide father", she explains. "So your friend joined you and Caledon", he inquires further. "I won't lie to you father. His name is Jack Denver. He is a guitarist and I met him in Mr. Charles wedding. He was called to perform with his band. I don't know when and how I just fell for him. He is a very nice guy. I want you to meet him. I am sure you will like him too.", she confesses. Mr. Theodore sits down, "You know Julia, when you were born, your mother passed away. She was the woman I loved the most in my entire life. I was upset on your birth but then I saw you and I felt proud on being a father of a girl child. Your eyes had a spark which could move mountains. Lets see what you have chosen for yourself, call him tomorrow 11:00 am at the golf club", he instructs. Mr. Theodore is a smart man. He walks out saying this to his daughter. He knows he has to say no to this relationship but he wants to say so in such a manner that his daughter doesn't feel negative about him. Julia is nervous and super excited at the same time She calls Jack and informs him, "Baby, I told father about us. He wants to see you tomorrow 11:00am at the golf club. Please don't get late." Jack is happy to oblige "Sure, love!

Jack is thinking about tomorrow's meet. For some reason, he knows that will not be accepting this relationship. He prepares himself for his first meet. Mr. Theodore is dressed all in white, playing golf with his friends. Jack is there to meet him. He meets Roger at the club, "Hey buddy, what are you doing here?", Roger greets Jack. "I came to meet Mr. Theodore. Could you inform him I am here? Jack asks his friend. "Sure, but for what? If I may ask", Roger is intrigued. Jack responds "Some work". Roger is more curios now, "Some work or is it Julia? You know she is Candy's friend. Candy was telling me you guys gelled pretty well". "I'll tell you later. For now, I have to see Mr. Theodore. If you could tell him I am here, it will be really nice. Roger obliges, "Sure, come along!" Roger walks on to the golf ground with Jack.

Roger intervenes "Mr. Theodore, there is a guest to see you. Jack Denver". Mr. Theodore turns around and looks at Jack. He hands over the golf club to one of the attendants standing close and takes the cigar from other. He walk towards Jack, Jack introduces himself, "Hello Sir, I am Jack Denver, nice to meet you." Mr. Theodore looks at him top to toe. He takes the first puff and says, "Jack Denver the guitarist and main singer for the band EBO. Jack who doesn't have a father and mother. Jack who has a younger brother John and stays with his uncle and aunt". Jack is shocked but calm "That is right sir". Mr. Theodore takes another puff, "There is one more thing that is right Denver. Your excellent plan of making my daughter fall in love with you, and then achieve all the success in life. What an amazing shortcut to be successful". Jack is offended, "Sorry, Mr. Theodore but.." Mr. Theodore cuts him off, "You should be sorry. Sorry for manipulating my daughter. Sorry for making my guest Mr. Caledon eat horse feed pounce. He has been so unwell because of this mischief of yours. What did you think? This is something very cool you have done. You know I can throw you behind bars for this act. You pretended to be a guide, faked your identity". Jack is uncomfortable, "Mr. Theodore, I love your daughter and I don't care what you do or you want to do. I am here to see you because Julia wanted me to. Yes, I am a very small person in front of you, but I don't have a narrow mentality to trade love for money. I loved her without knowing that she was a daughter of an industrialist. And I will continue to do so. I am a fighter and I don't wish to get anything from you except your daughter. If you will happily give her hand to me, it will be wonderful for all. If you don't, I will still marry her, with or without you". Mr. Theodore is equal in his response "Have you even seen yourself? How much do you make in a month? My daughter will have a lavish wedding. Can you even afford her a pair of Jimmy Choo? Just look at yourself and look at her. You are so ordinary and she is a woman of poise and grace. You are not even an atom close to her standards". Jack smiles at Mr. Theodore and says "I am glad I am an atom. It's good to know from you that you consider my existence at least. Thank you for your time sir, I shall make myself big enough that I can buy her Jimmy Choo. Till then Julia is my treasure with you. Keep her safe. I will show my end of loyalty and you will show yours".

Mr. Theodore smiles with arrogance while Jack walks away. Roger stops Jack, "Hey seems like the meeting was not good. Come on Jack, you can tell me. We are friends dude. The last time you know I was into Candy man and everything is fair in love and war". "What do you want to know? I met Theodore because I am seeing Julia and we want to get married. "Woah woah woah, that was quick. You just met her and now it is true love and all. "I need to go Roger. I have a lot to do", Jack says, brushing past his friend. "Theodore is an arrogant man. He won't give his daughter's hand to someone so ordinary like you", Roger reminds him. "Tell me something I don't know", says Jack as he walks away. "He has already chosen Caledon for her", Roger screams out. Jack stops on the way and looks back at Roger. Roger takes few steps towards him. "How can you be so sure?", asks Jack. "Theodore was speaking to Candy's father. He told him he has found the right match for his daughter. He is the investor in his upcoming projects as well. Jack, this will not be easy for you. But it's not impossible. Let me speak to Candy. She has lot of contacts. Maybe we can do something for you", Roger says and gives him a hug.

Jack is walking back home, thinking if Mr. Theodore, has already made up his mind on Caledon. He will not really care for his efforts. Julia calls him on the way," Baby, how was your first meet? I hope he didn't grill you much", she says hopefully. "Hmmm it was good", he says curtly. "Are you ok? Did he say something?", she asks. "Yes all good!" "Why don't you sound good.?" Jack is distracted "Babe, can I call you later?" "Sure, please take care", she hangs up with those words.

Julia calls her father without wasting a minute. "Father, how was your meeting with Jack, did you like him?", she asks. "It was ok. He is not settled at the moment Julia, yet for your happiness sake, I have given him a fair chance to prove himself". "Father, what do you mean by that?", she asks. "Dear I have earned this name, respect and luxury. People across globe know me. For me to give my daughter's hand to someone who is not even earning a fixed salary for a month is certainly an area of concern. Love is beautiful but I believe in the practicality. Let's see what he is after a year and then we shall talk about it. Mr. Theodore hangs up. Julia is upset with her father's decision. Now she knows what has upset Jack. She calls him and insists on meeting. But Jack doesn't want to. He needed his space for some time.

Mr. Theodore, on the other hand, asks Julia to checkout from the hotel as they are to go back to Edinburgh from this short vacation. He sends the chauffer, who takes Caledon and Julia back to Edinburgh. Caledon tried talking to Julia on the way many times, but she was so lost. She didn't even get to meet Jack before leaving and her disappointment was natural. Roger informs

Jack that Mr. Theodore along with Caledon and Julia have left for Edinburgh. Jack plays with his brother. He misses Julia. He wants to call her but he has nothing to say. Julia tried to reach him but there was no response. Candy visits Julia on her return from North Berwick. Roger has already disclosed everything to her. She reaches out to Julia like a support system as always.

"I know everything. You need to have faith and you know people do fall apart to get back stronger with each other. And it is normal", she reassures Julia. "Father doesn't like him. He will never accept him and probably Jack is convinced about it, hence he isn't picking my calls or answering my messages", she cries as she says this. "Babe, he is going through stress himself. you need to think positive and allow him time to get back to you. Till then you focus on work and let us see how best we can support him in getting where your father wants him to be", she suggests. Julia pauses,"That makes so much of a sense". "Well, I am a sensible girl!"Julia and Candy laugh and hug each other. Julia joins back at work.

On the other hand Jack starts looking for the best opportunities for himself. He does lots of shows and gives many live performances. It took him 3 months to go public, and be visible as a band lead and performer. However, he was still waiting for one big pick that will change his life. Jack travels to different places. He is earning more than well for himself. However, it is not enough for Julia's father to get convinced.

A lot of time has passed. They haven't spoken from a good 4 months now. Julia is waiting for him to call, and Jack is so busy traveling. He is working hard to get close to his achievement. He wants Julia in his life and he is keeping his focus right, without realizing that she is waiting to hear from him. He writes a letter to Julia, and informs her that he is travelling wherever he can with his band, to earn that name and fame that her father is looking for in her life partner.

"Dear Julia,

I know you have been waiting long to hear from me. I am extremely sorry for making you go through this. However, I would need your support love and trust to achieve my dream which is you. I love you and I will see you soon. Till then, wait for me. I am away from you and it is quite a long distance darling. But our love is strong enough to fight this. Love, Jack."

Julia's eyes are watering. She has been waiting to hear from him from so long, and now she has his first letter. But she can't reply as he is travelling and she has no clue what is his next step.

# Long Distance

Almost eight months have passed since the time Jack wrote that first and last letter to Julia. He has been in no news. Julia is lonely and sad each passing day. Candy is looking for some real good opportunities where she can recommend Jack, however she is not getting anything big.

Mr. Theodore on the other hand is getting eager to marry his daughter to Caledon. He finally makes a call to Caledon. They meet to discuss business and in between the conversation, Mr. Theodore expresses his wish, "I am a father of a daughter, who wishes to give her the best. Cal, you are that one man I can see my daughter happy and settled with. I would like to ask you, will you be interested in settling with her and we can change this business partnership into family?" Caledon was a smart businessman he knows how much he needs Theodore's association more than Theodore needs his. He smiled and replied, "Julia is a wonderful girl, and it will be my honor to have her as my life partner. However, her happiness is equally important. I hope you have asked her before me". Mr. Theodore replies, "Oh don't worry about that. My daughter is very innocent. She doesn't know what is right and wrong for her. But I am sure my decision will not make her unhappy". They smiled to each other and greeted back with a warm hug. Mr. Theodore is happy, "Let us celebrate this and announce to the world the inauguration of our new project followed by the engagement and the lifelong partnership to our guests". Caledon is happy too "Sure, sir". They clinked their glasses together on this and spent the evening together.

Julia is at work. She receives a call from her father, Mr. Theodre. "Darling, I am reaching home and we will have dinner together tonight. If you have made any plans, you need to cancel, because I want my daughter to myself." Julia replies, "Sure father, I will reach home early and get your favorite meal cooked for dinner." They keep the phone down. Julia goes to Candy and informs her about leaving early. Candy wants details, "Dinner with father? I hope he is not planning to send you away". Julia responds "I don't know, but he definitely has something to share".

Julia packs up for the day. She leaves for home. Once there, she quickly makes the arrangements for supper. She supervises the chef in the kitchen, preparing salmon for dinner. Mr. Theodore finally arrives home. He hugs Julia, "My baby, it feels so good to see you after so many days. But what is wrong with you? Your face looks so pale", Mr. Theodore expressed. Julia smiled removed his coat and said, "Well you are seeing me with too much love, father". Mr. Theodore is not amused, "I am your father Julia. I know when you are happy and when you are sad. Any communication from Jack?" Julia looks down with no response. Mr. Theodore consolingly, "Darling, he will not come back". "Why are you saying this father?" Mr. Theodore pats her on the back, "Come lets have dinner and talk". Mr. Theodore shouts out, "Rosy please serve the dinner". Rosy prepares the table. She gets the red wine, followed by salmon and breads.

Mr. Theodore looks at Julia. He keeps his palm on her hand and says, "I am your father Julia. I want to see you happy. Jack will not come back. I want you to accept it now. I just asked him what a father should ask from the man who will marry her daughter. He cannot reach to our life standards. Just look at yourself and understand you are blessed with this life. Why do you want to go and live the life that is not made for you. He can never buy you happiness". Julia's eyes are filled with tears but she isn't allowing them to fall that moment. She is quite. Mr. Theodore, in an assertive manner says, "Well, I have given 12 months time to Jack to prove himself. 8 months have passed and the last 4 months are left. I don't have any hope of him returning. You should also move on now. I have met Caledon today. He is a nice man and most importantly he is a well settled man. And we are getting into business together. I know him inside out. He is the right man for you. I have given your proposal to him, which he has accepted. You need to be smart now. Not every girl is lucky to get married to a man like Caledon". Julia stands up and with a heavy heart replies, "Father, thank you for the lovely dinner. I have an early morning tomorrow. I will take your leave. Please excuse me". She cleans her hand with the napkin and walks to her room. Mr. Theodore, is in deep thought thinking as to what to say on this behavior of Julia. Julia reaches her room and locks herself. She cries a lot. She cries like a little baby the whole night. She looks at the picture of Jack in her phone and can't get hold of herself. Julia knows by now, her father will make her get married to Caledon. Hence, she decides to make it straight with Caledon. She calls him and plans a meeting.

"Caledon, Hi. It's me Julia". "Yes. Of course I know it is you. I can't tell you how glad I am to hear from you", he responds, visibly elated. 'Can we meet Caledon?", she asks. "It will be my honor. Let's catch up for lunch tomorrow at Nok's Kitchen around 12 noon. They make amazing Thai food". Julia agrees "Sure, I will be there". "I will send my car", Caledon suggests. But Julia is dismissive "No, don't bother. I will come from work myself. Julia reaches work and discloses this to Candy. "Your father is really smart. For some reason, I know this dinner had something else for you. So now what?", asks Candy. "I don't know what I'll speak to Caledon about. I think am going to tell him about Jack and Me", says Julia. "Hmmm, but don't forget. He is a business partner to your father. What if he gives it back on business terms to him. Babe, be sure about what you are doing. I will call Roger and ask him to find out where the hell is Jack", she says so reassuringly to Julia. Julia is looking out at the window, lost in her thoughts. She is blank with her eyes wet. She strengthens herself and walks to her work station. She closes all her pending work and leaves to meet Caledon for lunch.

Caledon is there at Nok's kitchen like a real gentleman, waiting for the lady. He has reserved a table close to the window with a fantastic view. Julia reaches the restaurant. She finds Caledon, waving his hand at her. She walks towards him carraying her handbag and overcoat in one hand, and hair open down on one side. Caledon smiles and moves forward to kiss her on the cheek. He pulls the chair for her and makes her comfortable.

Julia looks down, left right and center. She doesn't know how to initiate the conversation. So Caledon takes the lead, "So this was quite quick actually. I never thought of you and me, you know. Your father came and gave a marriage proposal. I hope you are happy?" Julia smiles with hesitation and takes a deep breath, "Caledon, you are a great man and I am sure father has chosen you for me for a good reason. But...". Julia, looking at the big screen in front of her. It is Jack on TV, performing live at the Tomorrowland music festival. Caledon looks at her and he snaps his fingers to get her eye contact back. "You were saying something Julia", he asks. Julia is looking back at him and then on the screen, she replies "Aah, thank you. It is important to meet. You know we barely know each other". "I am glad you thought so and it is definitely important to give time to each other. So what should I call for you? You like Thai food? I am so fond of Thai", chirps a jubilant Caledon. Julia and Caledon get into the conversation of getting to know each other meanwhile Julia has several other thoughts passing her mind. She couldn't say the real thing she came for, to Caledon.

She kept thinking for hours after reaching home, "Why will Jack not let her know about Tomorrowland?" Has he really become one hippy band musician? Did he find someone else? Different thoughts flash across Julia's mind. Next day, she leaves for work, after much of thought, Julia decides to share this with Candy. "I know where Jack is", she tells Candy. "Oh he finally called you, I am so glad", Candy responds with joy. "No, he didn't call", Julia tells her. "Then? What is it Julia?" Julia takes out her cellphone and googles the Tomorrowland event. She shows the images and names of the artist performing there. "That's where he is", Julia says. "Holy shit, that's amazing. He is performing at Tomorrowland. Babe, that's the next big thing. I am so glad he made it", Candy excitedly says. "Seriously? A senseless place where all the jerks from the world come and say 'eat drink rave repeat'", Julia has her doubts. "Hey, come on Julia, just see his struggle. It takes a lot to reach this platform". "Yeah I'm sure. He looks quite happy and probably he has realized what is more important to him", she says. "You know what I think? We should go there and surprise him! What say?". "I have lot of work Candy, moreover he has not contacted me, so why should I make any efforts on him? What if he has found someone else and he just doesn't wish to come back to me?", wonders Julia. "Babe, you are doubting him without talking to him. That is not fair". "I have to meet Cal for dinner tonight. Dad has called him home, so please excuse me now". Julia leaves. Candy is surprised with her attitude. Julia reaches home and starts preparing for the evening. She calls Candy and asks her to join in for the dinner.

All laughs at the dinner table, Julia introduces Candy to Caledon. "It is a sheer pleasure to meet you Candy. You are really fun loving". Candy accepts the praise, "Thank you Caledon. It is a pleasure meeting you too. So glad Julia invited me for dinner, what a lovely time". Mr. Theodore enters the conversation, "Candy how is wedding house doing?" "Great Mr. Theodore. Our last wedding was a headline". "Charles, I know and I am super proud of the two of you. Cheers to both of you. I am sure you will be excited to receive one similar high-profile wedding, and it will be more fun as it will be of your best friend, isn't?" Mr. Theodore comments. Candy is looking at Julia, "Aah, of course. I have been waiting for this day. I would love to make it special for my best friend. Julia is looking down while chewing her meal with no reaction. Mr. Theodore, calls for finger bowls, wipes his hands in the napkin and excuses himself from them.

"So what kind of a wedding would you like Julia?", asks an exuberant Caledon. "Let me answer that. Julia has to start shopping a month before the wedding, and trust me you need to buy her brands like Dior, Jimmy Choo, Versace, etc. She loves shopping you see and the rest, I will take care of the décor. I know her taste", Candy rescues her from the conversation. "Well Ms. Planner, you have certainly taken half of the stress. Julia will look lovely as a bride no doubt. I will get the best gown made from Dior also an exclusive bridal shoe on customization from Jimmy Choo", proclaims Caledon. "Well then you have certainly won her heart as Julia is very particular about what she wears. You know what I mean", Candy is on fire. "Totally and that's how a woman of such a renowned family should be. After all, its all about the status of two families", says Caledon. Caledon wipes his hand and excuses himself from the dining table, "Girls, please excuse me, I need to sit with Mr. Theodore for some time. Julia, I will see you before leaving". "Take care Caledon", says Candy. "Thank you and you too lovely", responds Caledon. "Not bad. He is really good Julia. Just the right man for you". Julia is confused "What do you mean?" "Nothing. I just mean it. He is your kind of man. Someone who suits your luxury life". Julia isn't happy, "Thanks, Candy, anything else you want to say?" "No, that's all".

Candy looking at Julia, "I think I should leave now. It's getting late". "Sure", says Julia without looking at her. Candy leaves for her place. Julia is gazing at the sky in her veranda. Caledon walk towards her and whispers, "The sky looks beautiful". "Yes it is beautiful and silent". "Beautiful like you and silent like your heart". Julia smiles."Do you want me to get you a drink, Julia?", asks Caledon. "I don't drink after dinner". "How about an ice cream?" "Sure Caledon, I'll get for you". "No Julia, we will go and have an ice cream followed by a long drive". Julia is looking at him with a blank expression. "Come on Julia, we need this little time together before we get married. We will remember this and cherish it for life". "Sure, lets go. I'll inform father". "He has gone to bed. It's ok, trust me. You are not required to tell him Lets go".

Julia walks out with him. He takes her out on a long drive, playing some soft music in the car. An ice cream parlor was about to close, luckily Caledon makes it there on time. They ordered a hot chocolate with vanilla fudge. Time well spent. Caledon drives her back home. He wanted his first kiss but Julia just leaves him with a smiling face, a thank you and a goodbye. "Julia, are you forgetting something?" "Am I? Asked Julie" "I don't know Julia". "Goodnight Cal. I'll connect tomorrow with you".

Caledon leaves, finding this a little weird. Julia just doesn't feel things are going right.

As time is passing by, each day haunts her about Jack.

Julia is at work, upset over Jack for not picking her call. She is yelling over few freshers on small petty issues. Candy comes to check on her "Babe, you ok? You need to keep your calm, they are new". "Yeah Candy, whatever". "What is it? Why are you so upset?" "So I called Jack last night on his personal number". "Ok, what, wow I mean how?" "Yeah you are right, how the hell I did it. I shouldn't have". "Babe, I didn't mean it. But tell me what did he say?" "He said nothing as he never answered my call. "Ok, he must be busy. "Yeah very busy. Busy from last night till this morning and now afternoon". "Well, since you made an attempt of calling him, please read the headlines". "What, what is it?" "Read it". Julia reads it aloud "EBO lead Jack Denver injures his hand by resting his palm on bed of nails on floor." Julia is upset and shocked. Candy consoles her, "I know you are feeling terrible right now. Probably this is the unfortunate reason for him not answering your call". "He must be in so much pain, I need to be with him".

She gives herself a chance and tries connecting with the show organizer at Tomorrowland. The minute the call is answered, she disconnects the call. And then, she takes a deep breath and reconnects her call but this time straight to Jack on his number. The phone is ringing and is answered. Julia is sad. She sings in pain,

*"How can I forget your love?*
*How can I never see you again?*
*There's a time and place*
*For one more sweet embrace*
*And is time, ooh when it all, ooh*
*Went wrong I guess you know by now*
*That we will meet again somehow*
*Oh baby*
*How can I begin again?*
*How can I try to love someone new?*
*Someone who isn't you*
*How can our love be true?*
*When I'm not, ooh I'm not over you*
*I guess you know by now*
*That we will meet again somehow*
*Time can come and take away the pain*
*But I just want my memories to remain*
*To hear your voice*
*To see your face*
*There's not one moment I'd erase*
*You are a guest here now*
*So baby*
*How can I forget your love?*

*How can I never see you again?*

*How can I ever know why some stay and others go?*

*When I don't, ooh I don't want you to go*

*I guess I know by now*

*That we will meet again somehow*

*Time can come and wash away the pain*

*But I just want my mind to stay the same*

*To hear your voice*

*To see your face*

*There's not one moment I'd erase*

*You are a guest here now*

*So baby How can I forget your love?*

*How can I never see you again?*

A tear drop falls and she sleeps sinking in her pain. He explains his pain to her. He has a severe palm injury. He was unable to answer any call that night. His phone was kept on silent and away from his reach.

Julia speaks to herself, "I am sure you are missing me too, as much as I am missing him. I don't want to give any explanation to anyone about your ignorance as I trust you and I am sure you are working hard to take me from my arrogant father". Julia decides to go to Jack. She gets her tickets done for Tomorrow Land and leaves without informing Mr. Theodore.

Caledon, is quite happy with his last meet however he feels something not very right from Julia's end. He calls Mr. Theodore and check with him but then he hangs up in the middle, deciding to give himself and the situation some time. He sends a text to Julia, "Thank you for your time. It was lovely meeting you. Looking forward to see you soon". Julia receives his text, but ignores it as she is busy planning her travel.

# Love in my Arms

Tomorrowland is an electronic dance music festival held in Boom, Belgium. It is one of the world's largest and most notable music festivals. It now stretches over 2 weekends and usually sells out in minutes. Jack has finally taken himself to next level. His band EBO has become popular among youngsters. His music is an addiction for the ardent listener. He has finally achieved his dream. Jack has been extremely busy. His life has turned upside down, from, an ordinary man, to a polished celebrity. Julia arrives in Belgium, she has her tickets for TL.

On reaching the venue, she stands straight, looking at the crowd, feeling so good about Jack. Julia tries to connect with the event organizers but they fail to make her meet Jack on the first day. She has been chasing him, just to get a glimpse of him. "Oh Jack please come in front of me once. I so want to see you, hold you, love, hug you", she says to herself. Julia's father is disturbed on the other hand. He has no information about her,. Julia has just left a text on her father's cell phone, "Dear Father, don't worry I am doing good. Need a break, will be back soon.

This text was sent before she left home, since then her number is switched off. They can't reach her location. Julia is all dressed in a baggy t-shirt with harem pants, going well with the festival. She somehow manages to go at the backstage and from backstage, she rushes to the green room area. Jack is relaxing in his room after a breakthrough performance and injury. Julia knocks at his room, he responds, "I am too tired. Can we connect later please?" Julia opens the door and gets in saying, "Are you sure you are too tired Mr. Denver to even realize that there is someone waiting for you, for your calls and messages?" Jack looks at her, "Julia! It's really you". They both get close to each other and she slaps him a lot out of anger. Jack can't stop kissing her. They hold each other and cried for long. Love is melting in his arms. "Jack I hate you. I hate you so much", Julia kept saying. Jack kept replying, "I love you my baby I love you. I missed you so much".

The night passed they made love to each other. After all, it was a long wait. Jack kept admiring Julia in his arms. She slept like a baby, calm and peaceful.

Next morning, Julia wakes up to a hot cup of coffee with breakfast kept aside for her with a note, "Morning, love of my life. Please enjoy your breakfast and get ready for my performance to start in a while your VVIP coupon is kept on the side table. Contact Eddy at information desk". Julia takes a deep breath, smiles to herself and quickly gets ready. She reaches the information desk and asks for Eddy. Eddy is Jack's manager. He addresses her well and takes her around the festival. Eddy gets a call from Jack. He asks him to make him speak to Julia. Eddy hands over his phone to Julia. "Hey babe, how's the morning treating you?", asks Jack. "It has been very loving". "I am waiting for you backstage. I want to see you before I go out there and perform". "Coming my love". Julia asks Eddy to take her backstage.

There he stands in his casuals giving autographs to his fans. Julia admires this moment. "I am so happy to see you like this. My celebrity baby". "I am sorry for keeping you wait, but I am so glad you came here. I wanted to tell you about all this, just needed lots of time to give you and share". Julia is looking down holding him tight. "Babe, give me your love and wish me a great performance. Eddy take care of her". Jack leaves to perform. Julia takes the VVIP seating and enjoys his performance. All claps, the powerful crowd and a nonstop energetic performance by Jack and his band EBO. He makes a track that becomes a worldwide hit number. Jack gets billion views for that performance overnight. In this crowd of people, there was a spoiler named Bradley Atkins, shouting with the wave, "Eat, Drink, Rave, Repeat". Yes, Bradley Atkins, the son of Jeffery Atkins, is there. While falling on girls for no reason and making noise, drinking neat with his other half of crazy friends, he generally looks at the screen where they were showing audience.

He rubs his eyes, finding Julia sitting there in the VVIP lounge. He immediately leaves and finds a silent place, he calls his sister, Candy. "Brad, so what makes you call me? What have you done now? Hope they have not taken you away in a rape case this time", answers Candy. "Shut the fuck up and tell me where are you?", responds a rude Bradley. "Why do you want to know that?" "Well I just saw your friend Julia. I had the hots for her and she is here in Belgium, so I wanted to be sure for you to not to be around before I snap her". "What is Julia doing in Belgium?" "Awww poor girl your best friend didn't tell you that. Well she is enjoying Tomorrowland. Looks like her taste matches to mine". Bradley keeps the phone down. Candy hates her brother for various reasons. She knew that he will possibly do something wrong or put her and Julia in trouble, hence she decides to leave for Belgium too. Candy calls Roger and informs on getting his ticket done along with her. She informs her father Mr. Atkins on precautionary basis and leaves for Tomorrowland. The two leave for Belgium.

Mr. Theodore notices the absence of Candy too. So he calls his friend Mr. Atkins to check on the update. He gets a hint that now Candy is aware of Julia's location. He informs the police to keep a track of her cellphone. Meanwhile, he also calls Jeffery and generally checks with him, "How are Candy and Brad doing?" Jeffery replied, "Brad is in Tomorrowland, Belgium. He called his sister too yesterday. You know how this generation is. They are so crazy over music festivals." Mr. Theodore responds "Hmmm that is true. I will connect later with you Jeff, I have some work".

Mr. Theodore is now sure about Julia's location. He calls his secretary and asks her to get his tickets done for Tomorrowland. But before leaving, he calls all the media personnel and announces the wedding of Caledon Hockley with Julia Theodore. A grand announcement for all. "I William Theodore confirm the wedding of my beloved daughter Julia Theodore with Caledon Hockley. I will confirm the dates soon by this year. Looking forward to your blessings and love for the new couple to be".

# A Business Deal

The morning newspaper had a lot stored for Jack & Mr. Theodore. Jack gets the news of two business tycoon families getting together in a lifelong partnership. "Here is to the beautiful Julia Theodore and a brilliant hotelier Caledon Hockley". When Mr. Theodore opens the paper and reads about the heartthrob of current time, Jack Denver, takes the world to next level with his music. He looks up straight and says to himself, "Huh musician from small town". Jack shares the news with Julia, who is happy to share his growing success appraisal globally with him. "Look what your Father has done. "Oh God, it is my fault. I should have said no to Caledon". "As in, you are aware of this?" "Yes, father told me he has given a proposal to Caledon and I did see him the very next day on lunch. Just to let him know that I am not going to marry him. But then..," "But then what?" "I saw you on TV and I was so lost my mind was not working. I just decided to come and see you". "It's ok love. I will speak to him". Jack kisses her forehead and comforts her. Eddy calls Jack and informs him there are guests to see him. When Jack asked who, he informed Roger and Candy. Jack asked him to send them in. They are happy and excited to meet each other. "Babe, why didn't you inform me you are coming here? I am so glad you are fine. We were so worried for you", says Candy. "She is my strong girl and I am glad she came to me. When I was unable to reach her". "Hey dude, you have finally achieved success. I am so happy for you man". "Thanks, Roger". "Yes Jack, though at one point I thought you have forgotten Julia and moved on", says Candy. "This can never happen to me". "So what's the plan for today guys? We should celebrate!", suggests Candy. "I have no performance today, but David Guetta is performing live and I am sure you guys would love to watch as I can't miss his performance". "Oh yes, everyone eat drink rave repeat!"

The four enjoy the evening partying together like never before. Sloshed and exhausted, from one party to another. Hopping shows crazy, the four friends, until the next morning, Roger wakes up to pee. He is walking with a bad hangover. Candy is still sleeping and Jack is snoring at one corner. Roger observes the room around getting hold of his senses. "Guys, what the hell did we do last night? Just look at the condition of this room. Where the hell are you?", Roger says. He finds Candy, wakes her up and gives her a fresh lime juice. "My head is turning upside down". Jack too wakes up with a headache. "What a crazy night!" He cleans his eyes, stretches himself. Jack realizes Julia is not by his side. He gets up, heads towards the washroom. He knocks at the door. When there is no answer, he opens the door. Julia isn't there. Jack looks everywhere. He asks Roger and Candy, "Where is Julia?" "I have no clue. She was with you last", says Candy. "I haven't seen her since last I saw her with you in the lobby", says Roger.

Jack rushes to the lobby. He is looking everywhere, goes to the receptionist and asks her, "My lady Julia was with me last night. She was here when we were heading to our room. I don't remember anything after that. Can you please help me? You know where is she? Have you seen her going anywhere?" Receptionist responds "I am afraid sir. I was not in the late shift last night. I have reported now for work. However I can check with other attendants working last night. Can you share her picture?" Jack shares the picture. Roger and Candy join him down. Jack calls his manager Eddy and asks him to check everywhere possible. Jack fails to understand what went wrong and how he lost Julia in one night. "Keep your calm Jack, and have faith. She will be good and we will find her soon." Come on. let's just check our pockets. May be we find some clue of our last night mess-ups." They empty their pockets. Roger finds a condom and left over weed from his pocket. Candy gets a lip balm and a ring. "This is Julia's ring but what is it doing in my pocket?", asks Candy. "I found a club band of Rocky's night club". "Looks like a great clue. Lets go there I am sure we will get some information, but what I fail to understand is that how the hell we don't remember anything".

They head for Rocky's night club. Jack informs Eddy to keep an eye and be alert on any news he gets about Julia. They leave for Rocky's night club, on reaching there the bartender gives a furious look to the three, "Hi can I see your manager?" "What for?" "We are looking for our friend missing from last night". "Stella there are some losers asking for you". "What the fuck?" "Hey what do you want?" asked stella. "Hi, we are looking for a friend she is missing from last night". "So go to the police station. How can I help you? "Well, we came here last night. So we thought of checking if you can help us". "Help for charity?" Jack is losing his patience "Do you know anything?" asked Jack furiously. "I know there were four of you last night until this girl took the other in the washroom and then I have no idea. I don't keep my eyes on people coming and going". "Hang on. I took Julia to the washroom and that's how her ring came in my pocket. Because she washed her face removed her ring and gave it to me. Yes I recall this happened" explained Candy. "Great what after this? Where did you guys go?", asks Jack. "We came out and I informed Roger that Julia isn't well. We need to go back to the hotel". "Yes and we came back to the hotel" said Candy. Jack moves out of the bar "We need to check with the hotel management. But before that, lets ask them to pull out the cctv footage of our exit". "Stella, you have been really nice lady. Can I request you to please show us our exit from your club? It will be a great help as we can figure out the time for further investigation". "Well, I usually don't entertain this but ok, come on you three". Stella calls her security guard and asks him to show the video recording of the time these four friends left the night club. It took him time, but finally the guard notes the time it was 1:00 am, when they left from the club together. Jack notes down the number of the black Volkswagen which was taken by the four. Jack to Candy and Roger, "We need to find out all we can about this car". "Let me do that. I have some spoiled friends in import export of cars here, I am sure they will assist us".

Roger calls Phill, "Hey Phill, how are you doing bro?" "Hey Rog, I am good, how are you?" "I am good Phill. Actually not really my friends and I are in a messed-up situation. We need your help." "Ask me anything except money" phil replied. "I am sharing a vehicle number with you, need the details about this vehicle and if you can get me the driver nothing like it" said Roger. "Ok, go on share the number" asked Phil. Jack dictates 1-ABC-003. Roger repeats the same to Phill. Phill asks them to allow him some time.

Meanwhile they reach the hotel. Roger looks for the manager and asks for the cctv footage for last night. The manager agrees and guides them through the security room. Roger and Candy decide to sit and note the footage, meanwhile Jack goes back to the room and searches for more clues. Jack unlocks his room, finding it all messed and dirty as he has left last. He goes through every detail from bedroom, hall to washroom and verandah. He finds an unusual locket lying on the corner of his room. This locket had an initial "B" with a mini knife hanging on it. Finding this a little strange as none of the people he knows he has met with an initial "B". He keeps the locket in his pocket, as one of the clue. Jack gets a call on his phone. Its Roger. He calls him to come down and witness what they have just discovered. Jack locks his room and rushes down to the security room. Roger shows him the clip where the four of them are together and taking the elevator for their room. They reach the room and all four enter the room. He forwards the clip and shows after three hours around 3:30 A.M.. There is a room service person seen coming in and leaving out with a bell boy trolley which is covered with a cloth. "Can you see this? It looks so unreal". Jack is confused, "Who called room service?" "This is not room service, looks like kidnappers who had purposely come. Yes it is a planned act Jack", says Candy. "And they took Julia on that luggage trolley hiding from all sides with a white cloth", observes Jack. "Yes, we need to speak to the hotel on this".

Roger shares the footage with Hotel Manager and asks him to call all your staff and check who went to their room last night. The hotel manager is a little surprised too, he checked with all his staff and none came forward confirming their visit to their room. Jack standing out looking at the traffic, when the manager walks to him and asks him to involve the police as he is unable to get this sorted. Jack is thinking with his hand in his pocket, Candy and Roger join him. "What are you thinking?", asks Roger. "I got this locket from our room, I feel this belongs to one of the kidnappers who have kidnapped Julia". Roger takes the locket in his hand. He shows it to Candy too. Candy finds it a little familiar. "Why this looks I have seen it on someone". Jack looks at Candy, "Please think and tell me". "Why do I feel this initial is worn by my brother, but the question is why will he do something like this. Yes it can't be him. I just think too negative for him". "Guys we should inform the cops now. It's been 24 hours to Julia's missing and we have failed to find her. We need to go to the nearest police station", says Jack.

They head to the police station. "Jack Denver" one of the cops shouted. Jack walks with his friends to the main reception and asks for a senior cop. He is introduced to Jamie Deck. "Hi how can I help you all?". Jack explains the whole event to Jamie. His complaint is well registered. Jamie initiates the search. He informs all the check posts to keep a close check on Julia Theodore who is missing. Picture is shared by them to all the local police stations. Jack takes his leave from Jamie hoping for a great support. Meanwhile Jamie leaves with his team to the same hotel for further investigation. Jack to himself, "Where are you baby? Please come back to me once. I will never let you go".

There is a screaming sound, "Help me, can anyone hear me? Please help me". There is a black cloth on her eyes, and hands folded back, Julia is all tied up and struggling hard to pull herself this place. She is confused and don't seem to understand as to why and what has happened with her. However, she is sure that it is not normal and she is in a soup. Her ears can sense someone walking towards her. The sound of an iron door getting unlocked is heard. A man unfolds her eyes to the darkness. He opens her hands and toes, pushes her back towards the wall and locks the iron door. He asks one of his attendants to slip in food and water for her. She shouts at him and tries to know why is she brought here, "Please tell me, why are you doing this? Who are you? Why am I here?" The man walks away with no response. Julia is observing the walls. They look so old and strong. There is a tiny window on the top of the wall, where the day light can be felt. Nothing else is much of help to her. It is a blank room with nothing at all. Julia tries to open the locked door, but it is extremely hard. She tries and tries, even attempts to break the wall but she fails on every attempt. Finally, tired and exhausted she breaks into tears, missing Jack and her Father. Remembering them brings a small smile on her face and she sleeps tired and thinking. After few hours, she wakes up and drink the water kept. It is getting darker now as the day light peeping from the window is not losing out. This is getting scary for Julia. She starts shouting for help, "Hello! Anyone there? Please help me, get me out of here, please help, help!" "Shhhhh.... Why are you wasting your lungs out babe? You know you are 100 kms away from your friends and boyfriend and there is no one here who can hear your cry", says Bradley. "Who are you? What do you want?", inquires Julia. "Well I am no one. No one great that you should know Miss Theodore", he says with a cynical laugh. "What do you want? Why am I here?" "You girls ask too many questions. I don't like to answer", says Brad. Julia doesn't understand what is going on. "Who are you? Your voice is so familiar", Julia asks again. "My God, good looking and smart I like this combination. Could my voice sound so familiar? Afterall, I have used a voice changer so I wont doubt you". "Aaah, who are you and why have you got me here like this?" "You will soon get to know everything".

On the other hand Mr. Theodore reaches out to Jack and asks him to give his daughter. "Where is my daughter?" "Mr. Theodore, I can explain". Mr. Theodore stops Candy from speaking with his hand. And question's again, "where is my daughter, Jack?" "Interesting question. Actually I think I should be asking you this. Where is Julia? And how did you come here finding her?" "I came to know Candy is here and so I knew that she will be here too". 'We have lost her since last night. I have informed the cops and doing a search our way too" informed Jack. "Lost her? You mean you have no idea about my daughter's location. Great as much as I thought of you, you are even irresponsible" said Mr Theodore. Jack walks away and takes out his smoke and starts smoking. Mr. Theodore is all ready to blame Jack for Julia's missing. He has given statement in media, "My daughter came here and now she is missing".

Caledon calls Mr. Theodore and gives his support. He calls everyone possible in power, to find Julia. It's been 24 hours to her missing and no call or message. "How do we know if it is a kidnapping or an accident", said Candy. On the other hand seeing the serious consequences of kidnapping Julia, Bradley feels not right about this kidnapping. He has a fear of being caught. He calls the man who has promised to pay him a good amount of money for this kidnapping. "Boss, I can't keep her for long. There is tight security everywhere. If by any reason I am caught, I will be in great trouble. You please transfer my money as discussed and take her from here". "Hold for some time. I am trying to get Jack involved in her kidnapping", says the voice on the other side. "That is not possible. He is a big star. She came to him. Everyone knows they are dating. Your plan is baseless". "Hmmm, well if I cannot involve him in the kidnapping then I can get him killed in saving her. How about this?!" "What do you mean?" asked Brad. "Call Jack. Tell him the location. Ask him to reach alone with $50 billion . Take the moolah from him and kill him" said boss. "What is the guarantee he will come?" Brad asked. "Love doesn't need a guarantee He will come" said boss.

After thinking much, Brad agrees to call jack at the kidnapping spot. Jack gets a call from Brad and he informs Jack about Julia's kidnapping. "Get $50 billion and take your girl from me. Remember to come alone". Jack is all furious. He informs everyone about this call. Mr. Theodore moves forward with a blank cheque. "Take all my money but please get my daughter back", says Mr. Theodore. Jack, without wasting time, leaves for arranging the amount and make a plan with the cops. He had his doubt on Mr. Theodore for some reason, hence he asks Candy and Roger to keep an eye on him. Candy informed Jack that Mr. Theodore has just left the premises and they are following his car. Jack – "Keep me posted. I am reaching to this location the kidnapper has shared".

He reaches 100km away from the city to a place with lot of dark and shallow caves. Jack shares the location with the Police and Roger. Roger realizes that Jack's location and where Theodore is heading looks the same. He immediately informs Jack about this, however he is in front of the kidnappers. They asked him to throw the money bag. "Jack, throw the money towards us and we will leave Julia to walk towards you". "What is the proof you will stick to your words?" "Don't waste my time Jack. Hurry up and do as I am saying". Jack throws the bag towards Brad, his partner in crime picks the same, opens and checks. The money is there. "What a bad day Jack. You were right. What is the proof I will stick to my words. See your girl for the last time" Brad said. He removes the black cloth from Julia's face. She is terribly scared and so want to run towards Jack. But Brad held her hand tight. He pulls out the revolver from his pocket and shows it to Julia, "See him final time I am about to pull this trigger". Julia kicks in between his legs and rushes towards Jack. Jack quickly takes out his pistol, and shields Julia behind him. He aims at one of the kidnappers,"When you shoot, you shoot, you don't talk" said Jack. Julia recognizes Brad. She looks at him and shouts "Brad, you kidnapped me. I am shocked". "Shocked?! You will be more shocked to hear the name of the man who asked me to kidnap you" Brad said. "Who is it?" asked Julia. And before he could take the name, he is shot dead.

Mr. Theodore is heading towards Julia and she rushes to him, "Father I am so glad to see you". –"I am so glad you are fine", says Mr. Theodore. Candy is in a state of shock, "My brother, I do remember he called me talking about Julia. I am sorry I feel so disgraced, Julia". Jack walk towards Brad's body. He pulls out his cellphone from his pocket, searching the last dialed numbers. He finds the name Boss. He calls on the number, phone rings around. He is surprised the phone that is ringing is with Mr. Theodore. He cancels the call and call back again. He keeps doing it.

"What are you doing Jack? What is all this?" asked Julia. Jack turns to Mr. Theodore "So you are Boss. The name Brad was about to take when he shot him, Julia" explained Jack. "Yes, that is correct because we followed him and Jack's location matched with his route" informed Roger. Julia is shocked, "Father, really you did this? You planned my kidnapping? It was your plan?" asked Julia. Mr. Theodore "Yes it was all my plan. I wanted to kill Jack, because I didn't like him. He came in between my plan, my business deal with Caledon" said Mr. Theodore. Jack held Julia tight. Julia cries in his arms, "Jack please take me away from this place". She faints while speaking. "Julia, don't worry. I will not let anything happen to you" Jack said. He held her in his arms and takes her out of the dark horrifying cave.

Meanwhile, police arrive and Candy is shocked to hear the conversation between Mr. Theodore and Julia. She walks up to her dead brother and slaps him on his face. "I am ashamed to call you my brother. I don't know what will I tell father", cries Candy. Julia is coming back to her senses. She drinks water lots of water. The police get Mr. Theodore out tied in handcuffs. Julia is trying to understand what is going on here "why and where are you taking my father?" "I am afraid to inform you but Ms. Julia, your father is responsible for your kidnapping and Bradley's murder, as per the statement given by him", informs the police officer. "What? No that can't be true. Father, please tell them that's not true" Julia Cried. Mr. Theodore is repentant, "I am sorry Julia. It is true. I am not a good father. I planned your kidnapping as I was afraid to surrender to Jack. He has achieved the success I asked him to. Your wedding was a business deal for me. I wanted you to get married to Caledon so that my business can grow. I am sorry daughter, for making you go through all this" confessed Mr Theodore. Julia is shocked and extremely sad to know this from him. She moves her face from her father to the other side. Candy nod to the officer "Please take him away officer". Jack holds Julia and calms her down. Candy and Roger too hug each other.

# Brand Ambassador

Julia, Candy and Roger are back in Edinburgh. Too much happened during this trip that left a bitter impact on all.

Jack had concerts and performances lined up. He couldn't join them. However, he has asked Candy to take good care of Julia and he often calls her and texts her. Julia is home and a little low. She is missing her father and unable to forget all that he said. How her wedding was nothing more than a business deal for him.

Days passed of her in depression, she took several treatments and therapies that did help her heal. Jack would make video calls to her and they would talk long. Candy never ceased to visit. In fact, she encouraged Julia to join back at work. Caledon decided to go and see Julia. He is well aware about all that has happened in Belgium. He expresses deep sorrow for all that she has faced. 'Please take care of yourself Julia, I can understand what has happened is quite unfortunate and unexpected. But you need to be strong and you need to be a forgiver. Your father is a human, not God. Please forgive him. Be strong enough to do so. Than shall you can move on in life. Else you will be lost and still, live in this moment", he advices her. Julia looks at him and she smiles politely "Thank you Cal! It means a lot. I have forgiven him. I am just sad as a daughter whose father is behind the bars". "I am really proud of you". "Cal, I wanted to let you know that I won't be able to marry you. I am really sorry". Caledon, chuckling, "I know you want to marry Hop Williams, the guide". Julia & Caledon looked each other and laughed. "His name is Jack Denver, Caledon". "I know he is a public figure now. I am happy for you Julia, God bless you". "Cal, you are amazing and I am so glad that you are taking all this so positively". "Well I am happy to earn a friend in you than anything else". Caledon takes her leave and announces the decision to call off his wedding with Julia in the media.

Julia joins back Candy's Velvet Box. Back to her grin, planning the weddings again, Julia made herself busy and found reasons to be happy again. After all this time, she had the love of her life by her side. Candy's father, Mr. Atkins, is silent and lonely too. His beloved son is no more and his best friend is behind the bars. He feels bad and good at the same time. A weird feeling really. Roger opens his institute of golf training. He trains not just golf players but also he has taken a huge ground for training horse riders and the horses too.

Jack has bagged lot of ads and promotions lately. He has become the official brand ambassador for various products and brands. While in prison, Mr.

Theodore reads the newspaper. He goes through the headline, Theodore and Hockley call off the wedding. The end of a collaboration between two major tycoons. And the minute he turns the next page, the headline said "Jimmy Choo announces Jack Denver as their official brand ambassador for the Latest Men Collection, Runway 2018". Below he reads the interview of Jack, where he has mentioned, "my would-be father in law asked me if I can buy her a Jimmy Choo. I wish I could share this moment with him. Father I am the brand ambassador of Jimmy Choo. Do I deserve your daughter's hand now?. I am really thankful to her father, as he fueled the fire in me. Today, whatever I am I owe a lot of it to him". Mr. Theodore smiles reading every word said by Jack and he feels proud of it. He shares the paper with fellow prisoners around him.

The brand launches one of the biggest event. Julia is there to attend the event with John, Jack's little brother. They both sitting in VVIP zone waiting for Jack to walk the ramp. Jack makes a stylish entry after all he is the show stopper. Presenting the magical runway collection by Jimmy Choo, the press asked Jack, "How do you feel?" Jack replies, "Why should girls get all the bling?" And laughed. "It feels great, my fiancé is fond of this brand and I am glad to be a part of it". They all applauded. Julia walked with John to him, "So Mr. Bling what's your story?" "Well, I have a very interesting story on how I became a brand ambassador. It should be a push for you to buy the season collection for your man". Julia laughs, "You are crazy".

Interviewers gathered around Jack and Julia. They were bombarded with various questions. One of them was to Julia, "Ma'am will you forgive your father for whatever he did?" "I have already forgiven him, and I really hope to see him in our wedding because he is my best man, and he will always be", she answers. Another interviewer asks "Jack, whom would you like to give credit for your success?" "My father in law. The reason may be whatever from his end, but at least I am here because he gave that fire in me, that fire of achieving my lady and celebrate her for life. She is the best achievement of my life". Another interviewer asks "So how do you plan your wedding?" "No compromises on what the bride wants. It will be a hell of a wedding for both of us" answered Jack.

They leave the event. On their way back home, Julia is quiet. Jack asks her, "What is it that has kept you so silent" "The wedding is approaching and I don't know if father will be released. He has a murder case charge. Mr. Atkins will make sure he doesn't come out of jail. I really wanted him to be a part of this wedding. You know everything goes down to zero happiness when I think of my wedding. I am getting married as I always wanted to, with the man of my choice, with the accessories, shoes, makeup and dress, that I desired. Never thought my father won't be there. Nothing can fulfill the happiness of an individual's presence on this day" Julia explained. "Well, that's how life is Julia. You don't get everything in life. You are blessed that you can see this dream. There are many women who open their eyes to the harsh reality of life, where marriage doesn't really exist for them. They don't have families, they don't know what it is like to be well dressed. They grow to serve and end their life serving" explained Jack. "So true Jack. I just realized it is so late" said Julia. "There is nothing wrong in what you have desired baby. People have desires as per their conditioning and current state. We can't change this dynamic of life. This is how it works, however we can always contribute in making a better tomorrow" Jack said. "You are right, but what is it that we can do?" Asked Julia. "Let's work together on an NGO that will volunteer in making dreams come true" said Jack. "As in?" questioned Julie. "Let's help the poor women's families by financing their weddings" explained Jack. "Oh My God, this sounds so good Jack!" explained Julia. "Yes, there are lot of women or couples, who can't afford their wedding. They have desires too, I am sure. Let's give them a platform where they can share their desires and we can be a support system in encouraging those desires. Let's give them heels to stand high and speak their desires" Jack completed. "I love you Jack, this is such an amazing idea, I want to start working on this from tomorrow. I will sketch a plan and figure out how to go about it" Julia said. Jack smiles at Julia, they kissed each other and finished the conversation on this.

Julia prepares the entire plan. She names her NGO "I DO IN CHOO". The NGO that supports women and couples to fulfill their wedding desires. In association with Jimmy Choo, the idea becomes a big hit. Jack and Julia's love story being shared to all, supporting so many poor families across the globe. They are blessed and loved by all. The idea has taken the world like a storm. There are rich and well-established people who want to volunteer in "I DO IN CHOO", for the cause. Jack has taken the right steps. He just didn't become a brand ambassador but chose to take the brand together and worked for a cause. He addresses this to all, "If I have the power and platform to make things happen, it is my moral duty to do so. Being a brand ambassador doesn't mean to just work for the brand by promoting it for people to buy. It also means helping the ones who can't buy or do something extra ordinary that it touches their heart. They create your own stories by making a first move towards them. I feel extremely satisfied today. Whatever I have earned has been the fruit of the hard work of everyone around me. Make a change, be the change". Jack and Julia made nine weddings happen in the cause, "I Do In Choo". And finally the tenth wedding was their own wedding.

# I Do In Choo

And finally, the day is here. Everyone is so excited, they have waited long for this day. Jack files for a release case for Mr. Theodore, which gets approved. Julia is unaware about it. She is busy with her preparations. Julia gets her exclusive wedding gown done by Dior, along with a tiara supporting her long curly hair. She receives her desired jewelry by Tiffany and shoes by Jimmy Choo. Just how she has planned, in fact even better than her initial plans. The wedding is organized by Candy's Velvet Box and yes, she is the bride's maid too, without a second thought. Jack wore a black Tom Ford along with Moccasins by Jimmy Choo. Their wedding is one of the most notable weddings, at a church in Edinburgh. Julia is all set to leave for the church, when she gives a thought to her father before she leaves, and suddenly Mr. Theodore walks in saying "Julia, my girl you look lovely!" "Father!", she wipes her eyes and run towards him holding him tight. "I am there to take my Daughter down the aisle". "I am so happy to see you here" Julia said. "Let's go Daughter. Jack is waiting for you" said Mr. Theodore. Julia smiles and in a slow pace walks with her father down the aisle. Jack greets Mr. Theodore from a distance, and he can't take his eyes off Julia. Julia is right in front of him. The father of the church initiates the wedding vows. The Priest turns to Julia and Jack "We gather here to unite these two people in marriage. Their decision to marry has not been entered into lightly and today they publicly declare their private devotion to each other. The essence of this commitment is the acceptance of each other in as a lover, companion and a friend. A good and a balanced relationship is one in which neither person is overpowered nor absorbed by the other. One in which neither person is possessive of the other. One in which both give their love freely and without jealousy. Marriage ideally is sharing of responsibilities, hopes and dream. It takes a special effort to grow together, survive hard times and be loving and unselfish. Do you both pledge to share your lives openly with one another, and to speak the truth in love? Do you promise to honor and tenderly care for one another, cherish and encourage each other, stand together, through sorrows and joy, hardships and triumphs for all the days of your lives?" Jack and Julia together, "We Do". "Do you pledge to share your love and the joys of your marriage with all those around you, so that they may learn from your love and be encouraged to grow in their own lives?" Jack and Julia, together, "We do". "May these rings be blessed as a symbol of your union. As often as either of you look upon these rings, may you not only be reminded of this moment, but also of the vows you have made and the strength of your commitment to each other. Jack repeat after me asked the father, I Jack, promise to love and support you Julia and live each day with kindness, understanding, truth, humor and passion. With this ring I thee wed." Jack takes Julia's hand, repeats the vow and puts the ring on her finger. "Julia, please repeat after me asked the father, I Julia, promise to love and support you Jack and live each day with kindness, understanding, truth, humor and passion. With this ring I thee wed." Julia takes Jack's hand, repeats the vow and places ring on Jack's finger. "Go now in peace and live in love, sharing the most precious gifts you have. The gifts of your lives united. And may your days be long on this earth. I now pronounce you husband and wife. You may kiss the bride". Jack holds her softly and kisses his bride Julia. Their love gets a phenomenal applause from the whole of Edinburgh. Julia says to Jack "Yes I Do". Jack looked at Mr. Theodore and said "I do in Choo". They all laughed. There is resounding clapping and happy faces around of all the friends and family. Everyone is shouting their name. Love is celebrated like never before. Mr. Theodore is showering his blessings to the couple.

Roger walks towards Candy and proposes her. He asks for her hand from Mr. Atkins. Happy to meet Roger, Mr Atkins ascents to his request. Candy and Roger, can't stop taking selfies with them. Jack's little brother, John is all dressed in a mini tuxedo and a bow. He is cuteness overloaded. His uncle and aunt join the wedding too, showering their love and wishes to the couple. Jack and Julia shares a small note of gratitude to everyone who has shown up for their wedding and the loved one's who has been a great support throughout. Jack addresses the crowd "Thank you everyone! It really means a lot to us to see your happy faces with all hearts". Julia continues "I want to add a special note of thanks to my best friend, Candy, who has been there with me in my thick and thin times. And yes, Candy you did made my wedding arrangements amazing". Adding up to their note of gratitude a voice from behind joins in, it is The Charles, "Jack and Julia, heartiest congratulations to you. I knew this man will win something big someday. So proud of you Jack. And Julia you look lovely darling". Caledon joins the party too raising a toast to Jack and Julia, "Attention everyone! I would like to raise a toast to this wonderful couple, who have surely made me jealous on various occasions. But yes Jack, you won her truly. And Julia, he is the best man for you. Good choice. It's your big day and I am so happy I wish I had the power to declare a national love day for your wedding". Everyone goes "aww".

Caledon gets an encounter with a gorgeous lady who enters the wedding. It is Julia's cousin sister, Camella. Julia notices the spark in Cal's eyes for Camella. She winks at Cal and says way to go Cal. Caledon approaches Camella without wasting a minute. And seems they click well together. EBO played some of the greatest hits, to honor their main man. EBO teamed with Maroon 5 and gave a surprise performance to Jack and Julia, they all danced to this amazing song,

*"I'm hurting, baby,*

*I'm broken down I need your loving, loving,*

*I need it now*

*When I'm without you I'm something weak*

*You got me begging*

*Begging, I'm on my knees*

*I don't wanna be needing your love*

*I just wanna be deep in your love*

*And it's killing me when you're away*
*Ooh, baby, 'Cause I really don't care where you are*

*I just wanna be there where you are*

*And I gotta get one little taste*

*Your sugar*

*Yes, please*

*Won't you come and put it down on me*

*I'm right here, 'cause I need*

*Little love and little sympathy*

*Yeah you show me good loving*

*Make it alright*

*Need a little sweetness in my life*

*Your sugar*

*Yes, please*

*Won't you come and put it down on me*

*My broken pieces*

*You pick them up*

*Don't leave me hanging, hanging*

*Come give me some*

*When I'm without ya I'm so insecure*

*You are the one thing*

*The one thing, I'm living for*

*I don't wanna be needing your love*

*I just wanna be deep in your love*

*And it's killing me when you're away*

*Ooh, baby, 'Cause I really don't care where you are*

*I just wanna be there where you are*

*And I gotta get one little taste*

*Your sugar*

*Yes, please*

*Won't you come and put it down on me*

*I'm right here, 'cause I need*

*Little love and little sympathy*

*Yeah you show me good loving*

*Make it alright Need a little sweetness in my life*

*Your sugar (your sugar)*

*Yes, please (yes, please)*

*Won't you come and put it down on me*

*Yeah I want that red velvet I want that sugar sweet*

*Don't let nobody touch it*

*Unless that somebody's me*

*I gotta be a man*

*There ain't no other way*

*'Cause girl you're hotter than southern California Bay*

*I don't wanna play no games*

*I don't gotta be afraid*

*Don't give all that shy shit*

*No make up on, that's my*

*Sugar Yes, please*

*Won't you come and put it down on me (down on me)*

*Oh, right here (right here),*

*'Cause I need (I need)*

*Little love and little sympathy*

*Yeah you show me good loving*

*Make it alright*

*Need a little sweetness in my life*

*Your sugar (sugar)*

*Yes, please (yes, please)*

*Won't you come and put it down on me*

*Your sugar*

*Yes, please*

*Won't you come and put it down on me*

*I'm right here, 'cause I need*

*Little love and little sympathy*

*Yeah you show me good loving*

*Make it alright*

*Need a little sweetness in my life*

*Yoursugar*
*Yes, please*

*Won't you come and put it down on me (Down on me, down on me)"*

Jack held Julia's hand, and took her away from everyone and kissed his bride. Julia asks, "So what next Mr. Denver?" "The honeymoon in the Alps my lady". They give a goodbye to all the guests and take a flight for the famed Swiss Alps of Switzerland. "Oh I have been wanting to make love to you in the Alps for such a long time. You know, this is one of my desires since a very long time said Jack. "What is so special about Alps?" asked Julia. "They are the highest and most extensive mountain range system that lies entirely in Europe, stretching approximately 1200 kilometers across eight Alpine countries from West to East i.e France Switzerland, Italy, Monaco,

Liechtenstein, Austria, Germany and Slovenia. We can call out each other's names in 8 different languages while boinking there. But we are going to France for two major reasons" said Jack. "And what are those two reasons?", asks Julia. "France, in Western Europe, encompasses medieval cities, alpine villages and Mediterranean beaches, which is just so my kind of thing. And the second is its capital Paris. Famed for its fashion houses. Just for my baby, how she will love to see them, I so know said Jack. "Oh, this is where you are coming from, I see now", chuckles Julia. Jack tickles her, "Oh you see, do you?". They laugh, kiss and hug each other.

THE END